SEBASTIAN ROOK

VAMPIRE Plagues

Heart pounding, Ben stared at Emily. The sound had come from behind her! She was on her hands and knees beside the gravestone, staring down at the ground in horror. Abruptly she began to shake. . .

But no, Ben thought. It wasn't *Emily* shaking, it was the grave beneath her! The earth was rippling. The groaning noise became louder and louder. Patches of silvery, moonlit grass began to heave and swell upwards. Then Emily raised her head and Ben saw that her eyes were pools of terror. This wasn't grave-robbers – this was something else.

Look out for...

SEBASTIAN ROOK

VAMPIRE Plagues

OUTBREAK

SCHOLASTIC

With special thanks to Helen Hart

Scholastic Children's Books,
Euston House, 24 Eversholt Street,
London NW1 1DB, UK
a division of Scholastic Ltd
London ~ New York ~ Toronto ~ Sydney ~ Auckland
Mexico City ~ New Delhi ~ Hong Kong

First published in the UK by Scholastic Ltd, 2005
Series created by Working Partners Ltd

Typeset by Falcon Oast Graphic Art Ltd
Printed and bound by Bookmarque Ltd, Croydon, Surrey

10 9 8 7 6 5 4

CHAPTER ONE

LONDON, DECEMBER 1850

The grand lecture hall of London's Royal Institution was bustling as people took their seats. Perfumed ladies in velvet fussed with their skirts. Gentlemen in black frock coats stowed their silk top hats on their laps or under their chairs. Yellow gas lamps shimmered and hissed high on the walls, and the over-heated air was filled with the low hum of voices.

"Here we are, Emily. Third row from the front, seats four and five," Benedict Cole said to his sister. He was tall and fair-haired, with quick, grey eyes and a quiet manner that made him seem older than his twelve years.

Beside him, Emily Cole hesitated. "But those seats are reserved. . ."

"Yes, reserved for *us*," Ben said with a grin. "Look – Sir Peter's even put our names on them!"

Sure enough, there were little cards placed on the red velvet seat cushions. A neat copperplate hand had written in dark blue ink, "Master Benedict Cole" and "Miss Emily Cole".

The Coles had been invited to the Royal Institution that evening to attend a lecture on Eastern European antiquities given by the historian Sir Peter Walker, a colleague of their late father's. Harrison Cole had been an anthropologist who studied people and cultures. He had always kept a keen, professional eye on his colleagues' work.

Ben knew that Sir Peter Walker had been travelling for the past six months in Bohemia, Moravia and Poland, gathering valuable new pieces for his collection. Now the historian was standing on the stage at the front of the crowded lecture hall. Long rust-coloured velvet curtains framed the stage, and a set of wooden steps to Sir Peter's right led down to floor level, where rows and rows of seats – about two hundred in all – filled the hall. Tickets for the lecture had been hard to obtain, and Ben and Emily had been pleased to receive a special invitation from Sir Peter himself.

Up on the stage Sir Peter waited patiently for the hustle and bustle to die down, his perfectly manicured fingers idly smoothing his luxurious, black moustache. He was a big, broad man with sleek dark hair, dressed in an immaculate black tailcoat and a high-necked starched shirt. A gold watch chain stretched across the front of his white satin waistcoat, and a monocle glittered in front of his left eye. On either side of him were two enormous display tables crammed with antiquities and examples of Eastern European folk art.

Ben stood aside to let Emily slide into her seat. As she sat down, she tucked back a lock of her auburn hair and peeled off her gloves. Her fitted green coat had been buttoned against the chill December wind outside, but now she unfastened the top button and fanned herself with one glove. "It's sweltering in here," she whispered.

Ben grimaced. "Not as hot and humid as Mexico, though," he remarked. "Thank goodness!"

Emily shuddered and the siblings exchanged a grim look. *Mexico*. The very word brought back terrible memories for both of them.

Ben and Emily had recently spent several weeks in the South American jungle, battling against, and finally defeating, the ancient and powerful Mayan demon-god, Camazotz, who had killed their father. Their great friend Jack Harkett, once an orphan ekeing out a living at the London docks, had shared their adventures and become part of the family. He now lived with Ben and Emily in Bedford Square – and would have been with them in the lecture hall tonight, but sad news had arrived the previous day: Jack's old friend, Molly, had died unexpectedly, and today was her funeral.

Molly had worked in one of Jack's old riverside haunts, the Admiral Nelson inn. Ben had met her once, and knew that she had been like a mother to Jack during his years as a street urchin.

The gaslights around the hall suddenly dimmed. Ben sat up expectantly; Sir Peter's lecture was about to begin! He watched as the historian strutted across the stage to stand in front of a large pink-and-yellow map pinned to a wooden stand.

"When we talk of Eastern Europe," Sir Peter began in a deep, booming voice, "we mean this vast stretch of land that extends from the Baltic Sea in the north – here! – all the way to the Black Sea in the south – here!" Sir Peter flamboyantly gestured to the top of the map, and then to the bottom. "This troubled terrain has been divided as the spoils of war between three major powers – the Prussian Empire, the Russian Empire, and the Austrian Empire. My expedition took me from the northern port of Gdansk in Poland, all the way to Bucharest in eastern Romania."

Sir Peter puffed out his chest, took out his monocle, and surveyed the audience gravely. "I found the region to be a dangerous place for the unwary traveller. But I went there unafraid, knowing that the artefacts I found would make me the envy of others in my field." He paused, looking faintly amused by something.

"Indeed," he continued at last, "I have heard my work is *already* the envy of at least one of my esteemed scientific colleagues." Sir Peter let his monocle swing on its little chain, like a shiny glass pendulum. "A little bird has told me that the archaeologist Mr Edwin Sherwood has lately scurried off to Eastern Europe in my footsteps. Of course we all know the saying –" he winked archly – "where the great lead, others will follow!"

There was a ripple of polite laughter from the audience but Ben gritted his teeth, biting back the urge to jump up and tell the audience that Edwin Sherwood wasn't just following in Sir Peter's footsteps! The archaeologist was actually on a research trip, culminating in a conference in Warsaw.

And I should know, Ben fumed silently, *because I saw Uncle Edwin off at the railway station last week.*

Edwin Sherwood wasn't the children's real uncle, but their godfather. Neither Ben nor Emily could remember a time when they hadn't known him. He'd been a great friend and close colleague of their father, and since Harrison Cole's death, he had become their guardian. He was a brave, resourceful man who had helped them defeat Camazotz and his vampire servants in Mexico.

Ben glanced sideways at Emily and whispered, "Sir Peter's such an ass. I wish we hadn't come now."

Emily reached for his hand and gave it a reassuring squeeze. "Don't worry," she whispered back. "It's probably just professional rivalry between two men who both want to be the best in their field."

"But I feel as though we're betraying Uncle Edwin by sitting here and not defending him!" Ben argued.

"We're not betraying him, we're *supporting* him," Emily insisted. "Uncle Edwin says that the more we know about the history of ancient civilizations, the more helpful we can be to his work. You know how he likes us to learn as much as we can."

Ben folded his arms moodily. "Well, we haven't learned much tonight so far, have we?"

Emily smiled at him. "Maybe Sir Peter's saving the best bits for later."

"For when we've fallen asleep, you mean!" Ben grumbled.

He watched as Sir Peter screwed his monocle back into his eye socket, swaggered over to one of the display tables and picked up a lacquered black goblet, encrusted with tiny chips of glass and metal. Its stem looked too fragile for his brawny hand.

"You see here," he boomed, "an example of 'encrustio' crafting, a technique that has been passed down through the centuries. The owner of this goblet was very reluctant to sell, but I persuaded her." He smoothed his moustache with his thumb. "If I want something, I invariably get my way. It is said that sooner or later everything falls into the historian's net. . ." Sir Peter spread his hand wide across his own starched shirt front and gave himself a little pat. "Certainly everything falls into *my* net."

Ben shifted in his seat. He'd come here thinking he was going to hear about the skill of Mongolian horsemen and the savagery of Prussian sabre fights. But "encrustio" goblets? Boring. He'd have been better off at home with a book.

He glanced at Emily and saw that she was sitting very upright, as if she had a broom handle stuck down the back of her dress. Her eyes had a glassy look that Ben recognized. He grinned; his sister was struggling to stay awake. The heat and the smell of the gas lamps was beginning to make Ben feel drowsy too. He blinked once or twice and tried to focus on what Sir Peter was saying.

". . .In the mid-seventeenth century Poland was once again torn apart by conflict. It suffered a defeat from which it has never recovered, and I couldn't help noticing during my travels, that this has made the people somewhat over-dependent on religion and superstition. . ."

Hiding a huge yawn behind his hand, Ben slid down in his seat and decided to let himself nod off.

Emily felt Ben slouch down beside her, and forced herself to sit up even straighter. She didn't want to fall asleep too. She felt that one of them had to stay alert. Sir Peter had specially invited them to the lecture. Afterwards he was bound to ask which bit of his talk they'd enjoyed the most, and she could hardly say, "The inside of my eyelids, sir. . ."

But it was so hot! Emily could see that the two attendants standing either side of the doors at the back of the hall were almost wilting in their thick red coats.

". . .we come to the highlight of my talk," Sir Peter was saying. "A rather fine trophy which I stumbled across in the city of Warsaw. There is a monastery there, a rather tumbledown place which has fallen into disrepair. The abbot was a mad old fellow who felt that he and his monks were the protectors of several artefacts that I was keen to buy." He patted the front of his waistcoat again and smiled. "However, I explained who I am, and used my not-inconsiderable powers of persuasion, and eventually the abbot agreed to sell me a particular church bell. I had it shipped back to England and sent to a blacksmith for restoration – at great personal expense I might add!"

He stepped towards the table and briefly rested his hand on top of something shaped like a dome. It had been covered with a length of purple silk, which Sir Peter now whisked off with a great flourish. "Ladies and gentlemen, I give you the Dhampir Bell!"

A wave of "Oohs" and "Aahs" rippled across the audience. The Dhampir Bell was a beautiful gleaming bronze dome about the size of a lady's hat-box. Gaslight reflected off its polished curves.

"Yes, the Dhampir Bell. . ." Sir Peter let his hand linger on the top of the bell. "It's a tower-bell, or *campana* as they became known. Possibly dating from the fourteenth century, it is fifteen inches in diameter and sixteen inches tall. It has been cast in solid bronze.

Note the slightly thickened rim, which prevents against cracking and also gives the chime a deeper, more resonant tone. On close inspection, one sees a line of inscription around the rim. See here, hand-cut Polish lettering interspersed with various religious symbols."

As he stroked the surface of the bell, a satisfied smile settled on Sir Peter's face. "Took me some time to persuade the old abbot to part with this, let me tell you! Apparently, there is a rather quaint little myth attached to the bell, and while the abbot claimed not to believe in it himself, he still felt that the bell was an important historical artefact. Of course, once he realized who I am, he was happy to give the bell into my keeping. The myth might interest you, though. . . Of course, most people would have been terrified when they heard the story, but *I* am a professional. It takes a lot more than a rustic folktale to scare me!" Sir Peter proudly puffed out his chest.

On the other side of the hall someone cried, "Tell us the folktale, then!"

"According to my abbot friend," Sir Peter explained, "the legend goes that sometimes the people of Poland fall victim to an ancient plague – a strange and deadly disease. When people are struck by this plague, there is no cure. They suffer horrible, painful deaths."

Sir Peter gazed around the auditorium, his left eye moon-like behind his monocle. "But according to the legend, their lives are not over. No! For these plague-victims dig their way out of their graves and walk the streets trying to kill people! The Polish call them 'lampirs'."

Lampirs. The word had a worrying similarity to the word vampires, Emily thought, and shuddered.

Sir Peter chuckled. "Of course it's all nonsense! An intriguing legend of absolutely no significance to the *serious* historian. But if the legend is to be believed, these living-dead lampirs can only be controlled by the Dhampir Bell. *This* bell."

Sir Peter carefully picked up the bell. "As you can see, the restoration has been thorough. The Dhampir Bell has been cleaned and polished. Unfortunately, the clapper was missing from inside, but I've had a new part fashioned in solid bronze, and set upon on a yoke so that it swings like a pendulum inside the bell, as the original would have done."

With the clapper held delicately between thumb and forefinger to stop it clanging, Sir Peter held the bell up so the audience could see inside. The polished bronze shimmered in the lamplight.

"According to the abbot," Sir Peter said importantly, "the chime of the Dhampir Bell has not been heard for more than thirty years! Tonight, however, thanks to my new clapper, we shall all hear the wonderful, melodious—"

Suddenly, without warning, the heavy double doors at the back of the hall crashed open and a frantic voice shouted, "*Stop!*"

Ben woke with a start, and almost fell off his seat in surprise. Across the aisle, a lady gasped. Emily craned her neck to see what was happening.

An intruder had burst through the doors with such force that both the attendants had been knocked to the ground. One of them clutched his nose – fresh blood was streaming through his fingers like crimson paint.

The intruder stood in the doorway for a moment, poised as if to dash forward into the hall. He had wild blond hair and looked about forty years old. He was small and wiry, with an angular face and a long nose, and he was dressed in a dusty, old tailcoat and grey, striped trousers. His intense, pale blue eyes were fixed on Sir Peter Walker. "Stop! Do not ring ze bell!" the little wild-haired man cried in strongly-accented English.

Then he launched himself down the aisle towards the stage. As he ran, people all along the aisle drew back in alarm. The two attendants were now on their feet and they hurried after him, their heavy boots thundering on the wooden floor.

On the stage Sir Peter still had his hand inside the bell, holding the clapper still until he was ready to ring it. As the intruder came pelting towards him, he drew himself up indignantly. "Stop where you are, sir, or I'll have you thrown out of here!" he cried. "Guards! Guards!"

The attendants caught the intruder just as he drew level with Emily and Ben. They were burly men, twice the size of their captive, and they wrestled him to the ground in a tangle of knees and boots. The little man struggled wildly. Several buttons popped off his dusty tailcoat and went spinning across the floor. More blood spilled from the attendant's injured nose. In the confusion a lady screamed and fell back in a dead faint.

"No!" yelped the little man. There was the sound of fabric tearing and then the guards surged to their feet, hauling the man upright. He twisted violently, straining towards the stage and Sir Peter.

"You must not ring ze bell," he begged. "You will wake ze lampirs from their graves. . ."

Sir Peter tugged his monocle out and glared. "You, sir, would do well not to set so much store by folklore and myth!"

"It is no myth," cried the little man, desperately. "Lampirs are all too real!"

"I've heard quite enough about lampirs," Sir Peter spluttered. "Now, no more of this superstitious nonsense."

He held the Dhampir Bell up high and prepared to let the clapper swing.

"*No!*" The little man gave a last, valiant struggle and twisted free of his guards. With a defiant cry, he lunged at Sir Peter.

CHAPTER TWO

But he was too late. Sir Peter released the clapper and rang the Dhampir Bell.

The chime echoed across the lecture hall. The sound seemed to roll over the audience like a wave, eventually crashing against the ornate plaster scrolls of the ceiling. Emily was transfixed. The chime was beautifully deep and melodious.

But the little wild-haired man froze, his face a pale mask of horror, as if the sound were the worst he'd ever heard. Abruptly his body crumpled, and he fell to the floor in front of the stage with his hands over his face. "What haf you done?" he whispered hoarsely.

"I have done," Sir Peter declared proudly, "something which has not been done for almost thirty years! I have *rung* the Dhampir Bell." Turning to the institution attendants he barked, "Rid us of this lunatic immediately. I have a lecture to finish."

The little man offered no resistance when the guards

picked him up, and they had to half-carry, half-drag his limp body all the way down the aisle to the doors. Emily watched, full of pity. The man seemed almost broken by the bell's chime. The rest of the audience, however, was obviously mesmerized. People's faces were rapt, as if they'd had a religious experience. And the bell *had* made a remarkable sound, Emily admitted to herself. The chime seemed to reverberate around the room long after Sir Peter had put the bell back on to the table.

Emily looked at Ben. "What was all that about?" she whispered.

"No idea," her brother replied. Then he added with a grin, "But it was the most interesting thing about the whole lecture!" and he slipped back down in his seat.

"Don't go to sleep again. . ." Emily began.

But it was too late. Ben had already nodded off.

Emily sighed and settled down to listen to Sir Peter.

The rest of the lecture passed without incident. Afterwards, people lingered in the Royal Institution's grand entrance hall, sipping tea or glasses of cold lime sherbet as they admired the artefacts that lined the walls. There were clocks and chronometers in shiny wooden cases, bronze busts of famous inventors, and framed portraits of engineers like George and Robert Stephenson with their "Rocket" steam engine. The floor was a chequerboard of black and white tiles, and elegant green palms stirred in the warm air as people mingled, chattering about Sir Peter's lecture. There was no sign of the intruder who had interrupted the talk.

Ben grabbed two glasses of sherbet from a passing waiter and steered Emily over to a quiet corner in the shade of a potted palm tree. "Thank goodness that's over," he said. "I thought Sir Peter was going to drone on all night!"

"He's not the most interesting speaker I've ever heard," Emily agreed. She raised her frosted glass and gave the contents a little swirl. "Let's drink up quickly and get out of here."

But as they turned to go, Sir Peter Walker appeared in front of them, a mournful expression on his pale face. The monocle made his left eye look slightly bigger than his right.

"My dear Benedict!" he boomed. "Thank you so much for coming tonight. Your presence meant a lot to me, my boy. I am only sorry that your father could not be here. His death is a sad loss to the world of science and human endeavour." Sir Peter shook his head. "I extend my condolences to you at this difficult time." He glanced at Emily and added hastily, "And to your sister, of course!"

Turning back to Ben, Sir Peter continued. "So, my boy. Tell me, which was your favourite part of my lecture?"

Emily bit back a grin at the expression of utter panic that crossed her brother's face. She placed her hand on Sir Peter's arm and said firmly, "The whole talk was fascinating, but I wanted to ask you about that man who burst in and caused such a disturbance. Do you have any idea who he was?"

Sir Peter snorted. "A madman, that's who he was, my dear girl. Probably a lunatic escaped from the Bedlam Hospital for the Criminally Insane. But you have nothing to fear." He reached out and patted her on the head as if to reassure her. "Don't you worry your pretty little head about such matters. That tale about the bell is mere superstition. An intriguing legend created by a nation of primitive people who have nothing better to do than spook each other with strange tales!"

Emily ducked away as the historian's hand hovered over her head again, and Sir Peter turned his attention to Ben. He clapped him on the back so hard that Ben lurched a step forwards.

"You know all about primitive people, don't you, Benedict, eh? I've heard all about your travels in South America. Gracious me, if there's one place that's primitive, that is it!"

"On the contrary, sir," began Ben. "The people we met in Mexico were far from primitive. Did you know the Ancient Mayans carved an empire from—?"

But Sir Peter was waving Ben's words away. "Next time you fancy a spot of globe-trotting, you come to me!" he declared firmly. "I'll take you somewhere far more exciting than anywhere Edwin Sherwood's been. How about India, eh? Can't get much more exciting than seeing the palace of a maharajah. . ."

Emily and Ben exchanged a look. "Actually, sir," Ben replied, "we had more than enough excitement in Mexico."

Sir Peter was instantly contrite. "Of course, dear boy, of course. Forgive me, I get carried away with my subject and forget everything else. God rest your poor father's soul." He closed his eyes for a moment as if saying a small prayer, then continued, "And, Benedict, I beg you to remember, your father and I were colleagues, and I like to imagine that there was friendship between us as well. In the name of that friendship, I'd like to extend an invitation to you," he glanced nervously at Emily and added quickly, "*and* to your dear sister, of course." With a little bow he turned back to Ben. "If ever you feel the need to escape the hubbub of London, you have only to ask," he said conspiratorially. "I have a rather grand country estate out near Windsor in Berkshire. The journey's a mere nothing since they extended the railway last year. Your father was a guest of mine at Brayleigh Court once or twice, so perhaps you'd do me the honour of paying a visit too. Indeed, you could take a look at some of my collection. I've a rather fine piece that I brought back from my travels in the Ottoman Empire last year. . ." And he was off again, smoothing his sleek moustache as he explained how clever he'd been in the marketplaces of Istanbul.

Emily saw Ben's eyes glaze over and felt a wave of

17

relief when a woman in green silk sailed over and clasped the historian's hand.

"Pietro!" she trilled in a strong Italian accent. "*Magnifico*, my darling man."

"Ah, Contessa..." Sir Peter bent low over the contessa's hand and pressed his lips to her rings.

Emily widened her eyes at Ben. He caught her meaningful look and together they seized the opportunity to steal away, slipping their empty sherbet glasses on to a waiter's tray as they made a beeline for the door.

Sir Peter didn't notice them go. He was telling the contessa a story about his recent purchase of a curved sword. "Believed to have been Genghis Khan's own sabre, you know..."

The doorman held the door wide and tipped his hat to Emily and Ben. "G'night, sir. G'night, miss."

Moments later they were outside in the crisp, cold evening air. The Royal Institution was in the heart of fashionable Mayfair, and the streets were alive even in the middle of the evening. Glowing gaslights shone from the windows of tall buildings, pushing back the thick London fog. Horse-drawn carriages rattled across the cobbles, offering quick glimpses of soft, cushioned interiors and comfortable ladies in satin skirts, while, on the pavement, gentlemen in stovepipe hats hurried past, eager to reach their clubs.

As they made their way down the Institution's front steps, Ben nudged Emily and puffed his chest out in an impression of Sir Peter. "If you ever feel the need to escape the hubbub of London, you have only to ask!" he boomed in a pompous voice, sounding uncannily like the historian. "I've a rather grand country estate. The journey's a mere nothing. . ."

Then he was Ben again, laughing so much that his breath came in steamy clouds. "Em, if I ever decide I want to get away from all this, please remind me that I'd rather saw off my own leg with a bread knife than go to stay with Sir Peter at Brayleigh Court!"

Emily grinned. "I don't think he actually wanted us to take him up on the offer," she said, pulling on her gloves. "He only invited us so he could show off about his precious 'collection'."

"And don't we know what Uncle Edwin would say about that!"

"Uncle Edwin would roll his eyes," Emily replied with a smile, "and complain that Sir Peter is nothing but a pompous ass pretending to be a real historian."

"Now that we've seen Sir Peter in action, I can see Uncle Edwin's point," Ben commented, rubbing his cold hands together. "He was more interested in telling everybody how brave he was, than in giving us any information about Eastern Europe. Heaven knows how he's become so famous."

"Some of his lecture was interesting," Emily mused. "I thought the bit about the Dhampir Bell was fascinating."

"I just hope that Sir Peter is right about the

plague being nothing more than a myth," Ben said quietly.

Emily nodded, and then she shivered. "Come on," she said. "It's too cold to stand about out here. Let's go home."

Ben raised his hand to flag down a passing hansom cab, one of the thousands of two-wheeled carriages-for-hire which clattered through the cobbled streets at all hours of the day and night. The driver sitting up behind the cab obligingly touched his whip to the brim of his hat and hauled on his horse's reins. "Where can I take you, young sir?"

Ben helped Emily up in to the cab. "Bedford Square, please!" he said, and the cab duly rattled off into the night.

CHAPTER THREE

It was dark by the time Jack Harkett bounded up the front steps of the house in Bedford Square. After six months of living with the Coles, he was finally getting used to the front door and being greeted by the warm glow of the gas lamps in the hall. But this evening, when the door swung open, Jack stopped dead in his tracks.

When he'd left the house at noon that day, the hallway had looked as it always did: a picture of Victorian wealth and respectability, with a grandfather clock ticking sleepily against one wall and family portraits in heavy dark frames hanging on the others. Now, however, the hallway was aglow with Christmas. Candles flickered on every surface, swags of evergreen dotted with shiny red berries garlanded the banisters and the stairs, and gold and silver bows had been attached to all the picture frames.

Jack let out a low whistle. "Now that's a sight for sore eyes," he murmured.

"Good evening, Master Jack! You're back then?" The Coles' housekeeper, Mrs Mills, bustled through the door from the servants' quarters, bringing with her the smell of freshly baked cakes. Mrs Mills was middle-aged and portly, and dressed from head to toe in her usual sober black. She had a reputation for being quite fierce, and ruled the housemaids with a firm hand. But she loved Ben and Emily dearly, and ever since his arrival at Bedford Square she'd treated Jack as one of the family too.

"Well, now," she said briskly, taking Jack's overcoat. "I thought it was about time there was a bit of Christmas cheer about the place. We won't be making a big fuss this year, what with losing the master and all. But mourning or not, you can't have Christmas without a bit of sparkle, can you?"

"Nope!" Jack agreed, with a smile that lit up his blue eyes. "You've been busy, Mrs M. This is marvellous. I ain't seen nothing like it before in me life!"

And he hadn't. In fact, if he thought back over his twelve years as a dockside urchin, Jack didn't think he could remember seeing anything that came close. There had been a holly wreath on the door of the Admiral Nelson inn, he recalled. But apart from that, Christmas had been no different to the rest of the year. Jack had still had to worry about how he was going to fill his empty stomach.

Mrs Mills chuckled and ushered him towards the drawing-room.

Even before he opened the door, Jack knew that she'd been busy in there, too. He could smell fir trees and fresh pine sap. It couldn't be... Surely it wasn't ... a *Christmas tree*? He'd heard some of the street-children talking about them last year, this new fashion brought to England by Queen Victoria's German husband, Albert.

Jack eagerly pushed open the drawing-room door. The curtains were closed and the room looked warm and cosy. A sparkling, shimmering Christmas tree stood in the corner by the window; its bushy green branches twinkling with glass baubles and silvery strands of angel hair.

Grinning with pleasure, Jack went to warm his hands in front of the fire. *This is the life*, he thought. Things didn't get much better than this. And to think that this time last year he'd been huddled in the corner of a rat-infested warehouse with only a family of fleas for company. He hadn't known what lay ahead of him then. He'd had no idea that there were such things as blood-sucking vampires, for example, and evil demon-gods. But in a few short months he'd travelled to Paris, New Orleans and Mexico. He'd met a viscount, several sea captains and a world-famous archaeologist. He'd done battle with vampires in the underground network of Parisian sewers, learned to shin up the rigging of a tall sailing ship, and tramped through a seething, teeming jungle. Pretty adventurous for a penniless guttersnipe from London's docks!

But however cosy and comfortable life got, Jack could never truly feel that the vampires were gone. Too many months had been spent looking over his shoulder, waiting for something to emerge from the shadows. It was bound to make a person jumpy. . .

Jack thought about the sprig of blood rose he'd brought back from Mexico. Even though it was dead and dry, it still had the power to kill a vampire, and although Jack hoped he'd never need to use it, he was comforted by the thought of it under his pillow at night, carefully preserved in a small sweet tin.

Jack reached for the poker and gave the fire a little stir, watching the sparks leap and dance. Then he tensed. He could feel a presence in the room. Stealthy footsteps stole across the rug towards him. There was a movement just behind him and his heart began to pound. A smooth hand slipped towards his pocket – and all at once Jack grinned.

It was Emily! Jack had been giving her lessons on the art of picking pockets, just for fun, in return for the long hours she spent teaching him to read and write. Emily had turned out to be an unexpectedly good pupil. Her hands were slender enough to slide into small spaces unnoticed – usually. But not this time.

Jack grasped her wrist tight. "Caught yer!" he cried.

Emily giggled and Jack found himself laughing too. His heart lifted at the sight of her familiar face. She had wide dark eyes, long auburn hair, and a little frown-line between her brows; a legacy of the long weeks she had spent poring over ancient manuscripts in their fight against the vampire god, Camazotz.

Jack's gaze met Ben's across the room and the boys exchanged a grin. "One day," Ben said, "you'll regret teaching my sister to be so light-fingered."

"Nah," Jack replied, "you never know when skills like that might come in useful!"

Ben came to stand by the fire, holding his hands out to the warmth of the flickering flames. "What do you think of the Christmas tree?" he asked Jack.

"I love it," Jack said enthusiastically.

"We did it this afternoon, as soon as you'd gone," Emily told him happily. "Mrs Mills said it would cheer you up after the funeral. So Ben and I went across to Oxford Street and chose the biggest one they had."

"It's big all right," Jack said with a smile, admiring the tree. "How on earth did you get the star on the top?"

Ben grinned. "Stepladder," he replied simply. "Only just managed to get it all done before it was time for us to hurry off to the Royal Institution."

"I was going to ask about that," Jack said. "How was the lecture?"

Emily wrinkled her nose. "Let's just say that Sir Peter Walker is no Edwin Sherwood," she said diplomatically.

But Ben was more forthright in his opinion. "He was utterly boring," he moaned. "I fell asleep! The lecture was supposed to be about Eastern Europe, but Sir Peter mainly talked about himself."

"*And,*" Emily put in, sounding outraged, "he patted me on the head afterwards as if I was a poodle!"

Jack laughed. "He don't know you very well, then," he remarked. He knew how much Emily hated to be treated like a little girl.

"What about your day?" Emily asked him, a look of concern on her face. "Molly's funeral, how was it?"

"The usual," Jack said soberly. "Lots of men in black coats and hats. A horse with a plume o' feathers on its head and the cart covered in black cloth." He took a deep breath. "I've seen burials before, lots of 'em, but it's a bit different when it's somebody you know inside the coffin, ain't it?"

Emily reached out and gave his hand a sympathetic squeeze. "Were there many people there?"

"Bit of a crowd," Jack said with a nod. "They got quite rowdy actually. There was another funeral going on across the other side of the cemetery, and a bunch of people were at the gates all shouting and arguing about something." He frowned. "Turned into a bit of a carry-on. Some fellow was standing on a box and stirring up the crowd something rotten."

Ben crossed the room and helped himself to an orange from one of the fruit bowls. "What do you mean," he asked, "stirring up the crowd?"

"Well, 'e was warning everybody to watch out. Telling

'em that dead bodies were going to start climbing out of graves and looking for people to kill." Jack grinned. "Sounded like a lunatic to me. Looked like one, too," he added as an afterthought.

Emily frowned. "What did he look like?"

Jack shrugged. "Little bloke with wild hair and staring eyes. Reckon he was Polish," he said thoughtfully. "You gets all sorts down the docks – Polish folk, Dutch, a few Hungarians." He smiled. "Keep your ears open and you gets to pick up a bit of the lingo. Yeah, I'd stake money on him being Polish." He glanced at Emily and saw that she had an expression of astonishment on her face. "Why do you ask?"

"Well. . ." Emily said slowly, "Sir Peter Walker showed us all a bell that he'd brought back from Poland." She quickly told Jack the folktale Sir Peter had recounted, and explained how an intruder had burst into the lecture hall. "He had wild hair and staring eyes, just like the man you described in the cemetery. He begged Sir Peter not to ring the bell. He seemed convinced that it would rouse the 'lampirs' from their graves."

Jack bit his lip. "Do you think your intruder was the same bloke that I saw earlier?"

"He could have been," Emily said cautiously. "Did you hear what else he was saying?"

Jack shook his head. "No, I was in too much of a hurry. I didn't want to be late for Molly's funeral." He sighed, thinking of his friend. "I'm going to miss Molly," he said softly. "It weren't fair for her to die so young."

"Did you find out what happened to her?" Ben asked gently.

Jack nodded. "Old Bill came over to me afterwards. He was the landlord of the Admiral Nelson, where Molly worked. Well, we had a bit of a chat and he said she were run over, out on the road."

"Run over!" Emily looked shocked. "What happened?"

"Seems there was some kind of accident, late at night. Molly had been washing up, see, and Bill went out the front of the inn to lock up. When he went back to see whether Molly needed any help, the kitchen was deserted. Bill thought at first that Molly had finished her work and gone home without telling him. But then he noticed a broken glass on the floor, and Molly's ring lying in a puddle of soapsuds next to the sink. . ." Jack sighed. "Molly treasured that ring. It was her grandmother's wedding ring – she were Polish too, as a matter o' fact. But the old lady fell ill and died a couple o' months ago. The ring was all Molly had left to remember her by. Bill said the only time she ever took the ring off was when she was washing up, and he was sure she wouldn't have just left it there. So he realized something bad must have happened."

Jack's voice suddenly wavered. "The next thing he knew, the night watchman was hammering on the front door of the inn, shouting for Bill to open up. He said there'd been an accident – that Molly had been hit by a

28

carriage, a big four-wheeler. Bill hurried out to the main road and found a crowd gathered on the corner. There was a carriage with one of its wheels off. The carriage-driver said Molly just ran out in front of him like she had a pack o' wild dogs at her heels."

"That's terrible," said Ben. He looked down at the orange in his hands and put it back in the fruit bowl as if he didn't have the stomach for it any more. "Poor Molly."

Emily nodded sympathetically. "At least she can't suffer any more," she said.

Jack dabbed his nose with his cuff. "Not so sure about that," he replied grimly. "I saw a few graves that had been disturbed."

Emily's eyes widened. "What do you mean – *disturbed*?"

"The grass looked as if it had been dug about and then stamped back down. And a few of the tombstones were tilted over. Earlier on, that Polish bloke had claimed that was evidence of his walking dead. But it looked to me like grave-robbers had been at work."

"Grave-robbers!" Emily went pale.

Jack nodded. "They dig up the bodies in the dead of night, steal the jewellery and the hair – and sometimes the teeth – then they sell it all on to the highest bidder."

"Teeth?" Ben asked, looking doubtful. "What would anybody want with the teeth?"

"They use 'em to make false ones," Jack said. "You know – sets of gnashers for people who ain't got their own."

Emily shuddered. "And you think grave-robbers have been digging up bodies in the cemetery where Molly's buried?"

Jack nodded. "Looks like it," he said. He shook his head sorrowfully. "I hope they leave Molly alone. She had a hard life. She deserves to rest in peace."

Jack wanted to rub his nose with his cuff again, but something told him that gentlemen didn't do that, however upset they were. So he said, "At least I've got something to remember Molly by. Bill gave me her ring – the one that used to be her gran's. He said that Molly often mentioned me, when she was working. Called me Nimble Jack. . ." He sniffed and tried to pull himself together. "Made me feel special, that did. And it were a nice ring, too. Look, I'll show you."

Jack stood up and stuck his hand into his pocket for the ring – but the ring wasn't there!

CHAPTER FOUR

Frantic, Jack tugged his trouser pockets inside out. The contents went spilling across the rug: ha'penny coins, a length of string, a twisted toffee wrapper. But no ring. Where on earth was it?

He glanced at Emily. "Em," he asked hesitantly, "did you. . . ?"

Emily shook her head. "Not me – but maybe somebody else picked your pocket?"

Jack shook his head. "I'd know if they had."

"But you always say that a good pickpocket can't be felt," Emily pointed out.

"And they can't – not by an honest bloke. It takes a thief to know a thief, and believe me, I can smell 'em a mile off!"

Jack began to stuff his things back into his pockets. He felt angry with himself for not having been more careful. The ring was all he had left to remind him of Molly. "Reckon I've dropped it somewhere," he said miserably.

"In here?" Ben asked hopefully.

Both boys began to search the room, but the ring was nowhere to be seen.

"Think back," Ben urged. "When Bill first handed you the ring, what did you do with it?"

"Held it in me 'and for a bit. . ." Jack murmured. He frowned, trying to remember. "Then the funeral finished and people started to drift off home. But I stayed for a while, looking at the ring and thinking about Molly. Then I tucked it in me pocket and came on home. . . No, wait a minute. That ain't right. I spoke to Henry first." He smacked his forehead with one hand. "The handkerchief! Of course. I pulled me handkerchief out of me pocket to give it to Henry! The ring must have been tangled up in it, and it fell out."

Jack looked up to find Ben and Emily staring at him blankly.

"Who's Henry?" Emily asked.

"Henry's an old mate of mine," Jack explained. "Skinny little lad – ain't got no Ma or Pa, he just had an old uncle somewhere. He used to come with me to the Admiral Nelson and have a bite to eat. Molly liked him. Said he reminded her of her nephew back home in Poland." Jack sighed. "Henry got all upset this afternoon because it was the second funeral he's been to this week. His old Uncle Jerzy died on Monday, see. Poor lad's only ten years old, and he ain't got nobody to look out for him now Molly's gone."

"So the ring dropped out of your pocket when you pulled out your handkerchief," Ben said.

Jack nodded. "And I know exactly where it'll be. Right by Molly's grave. I'll have to go back for it!" He headed for the door.

Ben stared at him. "What – now? It's almost ten o'clock at night!"

Jack shrugged. "I ain't scared of the dark."

"I'm not thinking about the dark," Ben replied. "It's Mrs Mills you should be scared of. She's not going to let you put your nose out of the front door at this time of night, let alone go running off to a graveyard!"

"You're right." Jack took a deep breath and thought for a moment. "I'll wait until she's gone to bed and then sneak out," he said at last.

"All right," Ben said. "I'll come with you."

"You don't have to, I'll manage on me own," Jack assured his friend.

"And you'll manage even better if I'm with you," Ben said firmly. "You know we work well as a team!"

"All right, me old mate," Jack said at last. "We'll pretend to go to bed, and when Mrs Mills and the others are asleep, we'll meet on the landing." He grinned and gave Ben a friendly punch on the arm. "It'll be just like old times!"

"Ahem," Emily coughed and stood up. "I'm part of the team, too. You're not leaving me out!" she announced – and she had such a determined look on her face that both boys knew better than to argue.

Ben waited until he heard Mrs Mills go past his bedroom door, on her way to bed. Then he counted slowly to a hundred, tugged on a warm jacket and cap, and crept along the dark landing to meet Jack and Emily. They were waiting for him at the top of the stairs. Emily's eyes were shining with excitement above her warm, red woollen scarf.

"Come on. . ." Ben whispered, and led the way down the shadowy staircase.

Moments later they were out in Bedford Square, running for the cover of the leafy green park in the centre. Dense grey cloud meant there was no moon to see by, and the only light came from the hazy gas lamps. Ben glanced back and saw that his house, like all the others in the square, was dark and silent, with curtains drawn across every window.

"So far, so good," Jack hissed, as they huddled under a bush in the middle of the gardens. "But the cemetery's nearly three miles away. It's a long walk."

"We'll find a hansom cab out on the main road," Ben whispered back.

A short walk through deserted streets brought the three friends out on to New Oxford Street. Several hansoms were dropping off fares, most of them gentlemen in frock coats looking for late night cigar shops or supper-rooms.

Ben called up to one of the drivers. "Could you take

us south of the river, please?" he asked. "We have to get to the cemetery near the docks."

The driver wiped his nose with a big checked handkerchief and peered at Ben blearily. "I can *take* you there," he said, "because it's on me way 'ome. But I won't be able to bring you back again. I'm going straight to me bed." He stuffed the handkerchief into his pocket and rubbed his hands together as if they were cold. "Feeling right poorly, I am. Can't seem to get warm. Even me fingernails have gone purple. . ."

The three friends stepped up into the hansom. There was just enough room for all of them on the narrow bench seat, Emily in the middle and the boys on either side. Ben knocked on the roof to tell the driver they were ready to go, and the vehicle lurched forward.

Nobody spoke as the cab made its way eastwards through the city. Jack was deep in thought, his face tense. Ben guessed his friend was worrying about whether he would find Molly's ring. Emily was muffled to the ears in her red woollen scarf, her gaze flitting over the darkened shop windows.

Ben sat back and listened to the sounds of London at night: the rattle of carriage wheels on cobbles, the clip-clop of horses' hooves, the distant laughter as they passed a tavern. Then all at once he could smell the river, dark and rank. They were sweeping across London Bridge towards the docks. Mist rose up from the Thames and mingled with the city's smoke to create a curling yellow fog that obscured everything in sight.

Ben shivered, feeling the damp air settle against his cheeks.

"Nearly there," Jack murmured.

Huge warehouses loomed up on either side. Ben could see narrow alleys and lanes leading down to the riverside; they looked like tunnels in the foggy darkness. The only light came from the odd inn or public house. The muffled plonkety-plonk of a piano echoed through the gloom.

Soon they came to a high stone wall and the driver cried, "Whoa!" as he hauled on the reins.

"Here we are," Jack said. "Cemetery gates." He climbed down from the cab and called up to the driver, "Thanks, mate!"

Ben fished in his pocket for some money and paid. As the cabby's hand closed around the coins, Ben saw that the poor fellow hadn't been exaggerating – his nails really had gone purple!

"Better get yourself off home," Ben told him. "You don't look too good."

"Ain't that the truth," the driver moaned. "Hope the wife can rustle me up a whisky and hot lemon – that always does the trick." He flicked the reins and the hansom began to move away. Within moments the swirling fog had swallowed it up.

Ben, Jack and Emily were alone. Silence settled around them like a cloak.

Jack shivered and turned up the collar of his brown cord jacket. "Right," he said. "Let's find Molly's ring. . ."

The three friends turned to face the cemetery gates. Huge wrought-iron curlicues stretched up about twenty feet, topped with sharp spikes. A chain as thick as a man's wrist had been looped around the middle of the gate and secured with a chunky padlock.

Ben frowned. "The gates are locked."

"Course they're locked," Jack muttered. "Do you think they want to make it easy for the grave-robbers? But gates don't matter to us, 'cos we're goin' in another way!"

Jack took them round the corner and down a narrow lane along the side of the cemetery. The stone wall, ten foot high, loomed over them. Cinders crunched underfoot, then small stones. Jack stopped.

Ben bumped into him from behind. "What's the matter?" he whispered.

"The wall's crumbling just here," Jack explained. "I noticed it when I was walking back after Molly's funeral. Reckon the grave-robbers have been using this as a way in. We can scramble over, one at a time. There's a bit of ivy on the other side, you ought to be able to grab a handful and use it like a rope." He glanced at Emily. "It's a bit of a climb, and some of the rocks are loose. Will you be able to manage it?"

"Of course I will!" Emily said, grinning. "I've climbed every tree in Bedford Square gardens. I think I can manage a bit of crumbly old wall!" With that, she bunched up her petticoats and twisted them into a bulky knot above her knees.

Jack went first, then Emily. Ben brought up the rear. Rocks shifted underfoot, and bits of mortar came loose, turning to powder and drifting away. But soon they were the other side of the cemetery wall, brushing the dust from their hands as they peered into the shadows. It was colder here, and darker too. The clouds overhead were solid, shutting out any light from the moon. An icy mist curled over the graves. Somewhere an owl hooted.

Ben and Emily followed Jack along the path. Weather-beaten tombstones loomed up on either side like rows of broken teeth. Here a tree raised skeletal branches to the night sky; there a stone angel turned blind eyes across the cemetery. But at last Jack stopped, and Ben saw that they'd come to a row of new graves. The freshly dug earth gave off a smell of dampness and dead leaves.

"This is Molly," Jack said, bending over the nearest grave. He went down on to his hands and knees and began to pat the grass that surrounded the grave. Emily crouched beside him while Ben kept watch. He didn't really know what he was watching for – grave-robbers, perhaps.

Ben shivered. Something rustled in the undergrowth and he told himself it was just a beetle. Then a breath of wind stirred the bushes. . .

Jack gave a triumphant cry. "Here it is." He straightened up and held out his hand. Something gold glittered on his palm.

"Put it on," Emily suggested. "That way you won't lose it again."

Jack nodded, and jammed the ring on to his middle finger.

"Hurry up," Ben whispered. "I think I can hear something."

They all peered into the darkness, but there was nothing to see except swirling mist, the foggy outlines of trees and bushes, and the shadowy, tilted gravestones. Then a sound echoed through the cold night air.

Scratch . . . scratch . . . scratch!

"Grave-robbers!" Ben whispered.

"I think it's time we were leaving," muttered Emily.

Jack nodded. "We don't want to meet their sort," he warned. He stuck up his thumb and made a sharp, slicing movement across his throat. "They see us – we're history. Come on, back to the wall, and keep yer heads low."

They moved stealthily back the way they'd come, and Ben heaved a sigh of relief when he saw the wall rise up ahead of them, the gap clearly visible.

"Nearly there," he whispered, and began to hurry.

He was twenty paces from the wall when the dense clouds abruptly broke to reveal the moon. It hung low in the sky, huge and creamy, like an enormous face watching them. The cemetery suddenly seemed as bright as midday. Ben froze, aware that Emily and Jack had stopped too. Their shadows stretched across the grass like spilled ink. Between them and the wall were seven or eight graves – and something else that was hidden by a tombstone, but which made scraping sounds against the black earth. Whatever it was, it was blocking their escape.

Scratch . . . scratch . . . scratch!

The friends exchanged a horrified glance.

"Must be more grave-robbers!" Jack whispered urgently. "Quick – hide!"

They all dived for cover. Ben found himself crouching behind a cold marble tombstone. He couldn't see the grave-robbers, but he could hear them. The scraping, scratching sound carried easily on the cold air. He sensed movement behind him and turned, expecting to see his sister, but it was Jack, his face pale in the moonlight.

"Where's Em?" Ben mouthed.

Both boys looked around for Emily. Ben spotted her at last, hunkered down behind a gravestone on the other side of the path, her petticoats bunched around her knees. She was peeking around the edge of the gravestone, frowning. The scraping, scratching sound was getting louder, almost as if the grave-robbers had come closer. A dull knock-knocking joined it, like someone rapping their knuckles against a wooden door.

Ben peered out from his hiding place. Beside him, Jack

craned his neck too, trying to see which grave was being robbed.

And then a low groaning sound tore the night air. A rasping, guttural, inhuman growl. . .

Heart pounding, Ben stared at Emily. The sound had come from behind her! She was on her hands and knees beside the gravestone, staring down at the ground in horror. Abruptly she began to shake. . .

But no, Ben thought. It wasn't *Emily* shaking, it was the grave beneath her! The earth was rippling. The groaning noise became louder and louder. Patches of silvery, moonlit grass began to heave and swell upwards. Then Emily raised her head and Ben saw that her eyes were pools of terror. This wasn't grave-robbers – this was something else.

"Jump!" he cried.

And Emily jumped.

She reached him just in time, because the ground where she had been crouching was suddenly torn apart. Fragments of earth flew upwards and sideways and a corpse heaved itself out of the open grave.

CHAPTER FIVE

The once-dead body shook itself slightly and stretched upwards, impossibly tall.

Jack stared in disbelief. *Not another blinkin' monster,* he thought.

A second glance showed that this creature was something altogether different to the vampires he'd encountered before. Moonlight slanted on to its huge form. It had once been a man, probably six foot tall, with broad, muscular shoulders and strong legs. However, the muscles had wasted in death, and the flesh had begun to rot on its bones. Ragged clothes hung in strips from its limbs. A hideous smell – the mouldy, dusty smell of death – filled the air.

The corpse stood still for a moment, surveying the graveyard. Its eyes had sunken deep into their sockets, and each eyeball was covered with a milky-white film that seemed to glow in the moonlight. Then it growled deep in its throat – that same rasping, inhuman sound that the friends had heard before. It sniffed the air once or twice and then stepped out of the grave with great lumbering strides. It moved forward into a pool of shadow – and then it abruptly vanished!

Jack stared, blinked, and stared some more. But patchy clouds had drifted back across the moon and all he could see was a hundred shifting shadows. Where had the corpse gone?

Beside him, Ben and Emily were looking for the creature too, their faces taut and white. Evidently they couldn't see anything either, because they both turned to Jack, wide-eyed with confusion.

"What was *that*?" Emily said.

"More to the point," Jack hissed, "where did it go? One minute it was there, the next it was gone." He snapped his fingers. "Vanished. Just like that."

"It can't have vanished," Ben said sensibly. "We must have just lost sight of it. A cloud went across the moon, or something, just at the moment that the creature moved."

They all stood up cautiously and took a look around. The graveyard was still and silent. There was no sign of a walking corpse.

Jack checked that Molly's ring was still safely on his finger. Then he said, "Let's get out of here before that creature decides to come back," he suggested.

"I agree," Ben murmured. "We've got what we came for."

All three of them took one last look around, then they hurried back to the wall and scrambled over it.

"Reckon we'll have to walk for a bit. I doubt if we'll be able to pick up a hansom until we get the other side of London Bridge," Jack said, leading the way along the deserted lane.

The others agreed and they began to walk, their leather boots crunching on the cinders which littered the lane. The streets surrounding the docks were empty, but as they crossed the bridge a rattling sound came from somewhere behind them. Ben and Jack both moved closer to Emily, glancing back over their shoulders. For a moment there was nothing, and Jack felt a flicker of unease. Had the creature followed them?

But no – out of the fog came a pair of old horses with leather blinkers strapped to their foreheads. They were harnessed to an old-fashioned hackney carriage, a lumbering four-wheeler painted a dingy green.

The elderly coachman was muffled to his eyes in a moth-eaten greatcoat. He hauled on the reins when he saw the three friends at the side of the road. "You want a ride back into the city?" he called out to them. "It ain't safe on these streets at night, you know."

"Ain't that the truth!" muttered Jack.

Ben grinned up at the coachman. "Thank you. We'd be delighted to accept."

The musty interior of the old hackney had room enough for six passengers and their luggage, but Ben,

Jack and Emily huddled together on one bench seat. Each of them knew, without anything being said, that they needed to feel the comforting warmth of another living person close beside them.

It was past midnight when they finally drew up in Bedford Square. As they stepped down from the hackney, the friends could hear the hollow chime of a distant church bell. Ben dug out a coin and tipped the coachman. When he turned around, he found that Jack and Emily were stooped over a small figure hunched miserably on the doorstep.

Emily looked up, her face full of concern. "It's Jack's friend Henry!" she whispered.

Henry was a skinny little boy with a shock of straw-coloured hair and a pointed chin. He looked up at Ben with a pitiful expression in his huge dark eyes. "Please, mister," he said. "I don't mean no 'arm. I just wanted to see me old mate Jack. I didn't know who else to turn to now that me Uncle Jerzy's dead and poor Molly's gone." He gulped and picked at the frayed cuff of his grubby jacket. "I'm scared."

Jack was crouched next to Henry. "What are you scared of?" he asked gently.

"Somebody's following me. I keep 'earing footsteps," Henry explained. "They're always there, wherever I go. But when I stop and look, there ain't nobody to be seen!" Henry quivered and shot such a terrified look past Ben and Emily, that Ben had to stop himself from glancing back over his shoulder.

Henry looked at Jack. "I heard Bill say that somebody chased Molly. He said it scared her so much, she ran out in front of a carriage. D'you reckon they might be after me and all?"

Jack shook his head firmly. "No, I don't. Molly's death was an *accident*, nothing more." He ruffled Henry's hair. "There ain't nothing to be afraid of, Henry. Really there ain't."

But Jack's voice sounded hollow, and Ben knew that his friend was thinking about the creature they'd seen in the graveyard that night.

Ben shivered. "Look," he said. "We can't stay out here in the cold talking about it. Henry, you must come indoors with us. You'll be safe and warm, and we can talk about all this in the morning."

The four of them trooped inside quietly. Emily hurried to light a couple of candles and instantly the hallway was awash with a warm, flickering glow.

Henry gazed around in awe, taking in the grandfather clock, the carpet and all the Christmas decorations. "Cor blimey," he said. "This is a right toff's 'ouse!" and he sank down on the bottom stair as if his legs wouldn't hold him up for a moment longer.

Ben smiled, feeling suddenly tired as well. He unwound his scarf from around his neck and unbuttoned his jacket. "What a night," he muttered. "I don't think I've had that much fun in weeks."

"Ain't my idea of fun," Jack said dryly. "What on earth *was* that thing in the cemetery?"

"I don't know," Emily replied thoughtfully. "But it can't be just a coincidence that a mad Polish man was talking about lampirs rising from the grave – and then the very same night we see a horrible monster dig itself out of the ground in a cemetery!"

"Do you think that was a lampir then, Em?" Jack asked grimly.

"I think it *might* have been," Emily responded. "But I don't know what we're going to do about it."

"Right now, we're not going to do anything about it," Ben said, glancing meaningfully at little Henry. "We all need to get a bit of sleep. We can talk about it in the morning."

"You're right." Emily stifled a yawn. "What will you do – make up a bed for Henry in one of your rooms?"

"He can share mine," Jack offered. "I've got that couch that's almost as big as a bed in my room. We can pile on some spare blankets. He'll be as warm as toast."

"Goodnight, then." Emily took one of the Christmas candles and shielded it with one hand as she climbed the stairs. Her shadow reared and flickered for a moment on the gold flock wallpaper, and then she was gone.

"Don't think there's much point making me up a bed," Henry said in a small voice. "I's too scared to sleep."

Ben saw the little lad look fearfully at the front door, and sympathy welled up in his heart.

Jack looked at the front door too. "We'll soon see if there's anything out there to be scared of, Henry," he said, briskly pinching out all but one of the candles. "Come here and take a look."

Ben and Henry followed Jack, who had gone to peer through the stained glass panels on either side of the front door. At first they could see nothing but swirling dark shapes, imperfections in the glass. But after a moment their eyes adjusted, and although everything was tinted in vivid blues, greens and oranges, they could see that Bedford Square was deserted. Not even a cat padded across the empty cobbles.

"See, Henry?" said Jack. "There's nobody out there."

"Come on, let's go to bed," Ben said. He began to move towards the stairs.

Henry continued to look doubtfully out through the glass. "All right," he said. "If you're sure. . ."

"I'm sure," Jack replied gently.

But, suddenly, Henry gave a gasp of shock and his whole body went rigid. "There!" he yelped. "Something's there! I can see it!"

Ben and Jack were back at his side in an instant, pressing their faces to the glass. Henry was right. There was something there! A dim shape wavered in the shadows.

It was an old man, very pale and gaunt. He was of

medium height and medium build, wearing a rough black shirt and trousers. He stepped forward out of the darkness, heading straight for the house.

Ben and Jack exchanged a glance.

"I don't like the look of that feller," Jack whispered. "He don't seem natural to me." He pressed his face briefly against the glass again, trying to get a better look. Then he grasped a handful of Ben's sleeve. "Run upstairs. Under my pillow you'll find an old tin with a sprig of blood rose in it. Quick, Ben, get the blood rose!"

"Blood rose?" Ben asked, surprised. Blood rose was one of the weapons they'd used against Camazotz's vampires. He was about to remind Jack that the demon-god, and his vampire servants, had been destroyed, but then he saw the expression on his friend's face.

Ben's heart began to race. "Surely you don't think that's a vampire out there?" he asked doubtfully.

"I'm not sure what I think," Jack replied in a steely voice. "But I reckon you should go and get the blood rose. Right now!"

CHAPTER SIX

Jack pressed his nose against the window. Dread seeped into his bones as he watched the figure cross the night-dark street and draw closer to the house. *Was* he a vampire? Had Jack, Ben and Emily somehow missed something in their defeat of Camazotz?

The old man stepped into a pool of light beneath a street lamp, and Jack saw that he had thin grey hair combed back from his forehead, and wide Slavic cheekbones. A flash of gold showed he was wearing a signet ring on the middle finger of one work-roughened hand. During his time at the docks Jack had seen hundreds of men like this, loading and unloading the cargo from ships which sailed in from the Baltic Sea – Polish men, Lithuanians, Latvians and Russians.

Beside him, Henry suddenly gasped again and pressed closer to the window. "It's my Uncle Jerzy!" he cried, his voice full of amazement. "He ain't dead after all!"

He let out a yelp of delight and before Jack could stop

him, Henry had darted to the front door and dragged it open. "Uncle Jerzy, you're alive!" he called joyfully. "Why don't you come—"

Horrified, Jack leapt forwards and dragged Henry back from the open door. "No!" he hissed, clapping his hand over Henry's mouth before the little boy could finish his sentence. "You mustn't invite him in. Your uncle's dead. That's not the Jerzy you knew out there! It can't be!"

Henry's body crumpled against Jack. Uncle Jerzy, meanwhile, had come to a halt at the bottom of the steps that led up to the front door. He tilted back his head, and Jack felt a crushing sensation of terror. Jerzy's eyes were sunk deep into their sockets, each eyeball misted over with a milky-white film, and his mouth curved in a terrible smile.

"No. . ." breathed Jack, his stomach clenching.

Jerzy began to head up the steps towards them, his evil smile widening to reveal perfectly sharp, perfectly pointed white fangs that gleamed and glistened in the lamplight. He *was* a vampire. But not a vampire like any Jack had seen before, because where Camazotz had had four sharp teeth, this new and unknown vampire had twenty, maybe thirty, vicious white fangs – a complete set of razor-sharp teeth that glinted ominously.

"Look at him!" Henry said, now trembling with fear. "He's going to come in the house!"

Jack shook his head and muttered grimly, "Oh, no, he ain't. Not if I have anything to do with it."

Jerzy was halfway up the steps by now, but Jack pushed Henry behind him and faced the creature bravely. "You may not enter this house!" he said loudly.

But his words were drowned out by a groaning, guttural growl from Jerzy.

Jack remembered hearing that horrible sound before: it was unnatural, inhuman, the same kind of deep, throaty rattle that he had heard from the walking corpse in the cemetery. Jack flinched and slammed the door shut. "Come on," he said, steering Henry towards the stairs.

"But what about—"

"Don't worry about him," Jack replied. "His sort can't enter a private house without an invitation."

Jack swallowed nervously as he became aware of a sound behind them: a scraping at the front door, like sharp fingernails scratching on wood.

Skreek! Skreek!

Slowly, Jack and Henry turned around. Uncle Jerzy was standing just outside the front door. They could see his silhouette, black and solid against the uneven stained glass. There was a ripple of movement, and then Jerzy's hand came up, curved like a claw, and again scratched at the door.

Skreek! Skreek!

Henry whimpered, and Jack took hold of his hand.

"Don't worry," he said grimly. "Jerzy can't come in to the house unless we invite him. Even vampires have rules."

"You sure?" came Henry's whisper.

"I'm sure!"

But, even as Jack spoke, something strange was happening. Uncle Jerzy's silhouette shimmered and wavered, almost as if it was melting. It rippled downwards until it disappeared below the bottom of the stained glass door panel. For a moment nothing happened, a heartbeat in time, and then something started coming under the door. A shadow. It spread outward like slick black blood, pooling on the doormat.

The shadow grew and grew. Soon the shape of a man was stretched across the hallway carpet. Then, without warning, the shadow reared upwards and became solid, blocking the light from the street lamps. There was a rasping, growling sound, and the shadow raised one clawed hand.

But it *wasn't* a shadow. Not any more. It was a vampire, with wide Slavic cheekbones and milky-white eyeballs.

Jack stared, hardly able to believe his eyes. Uncle Jerzy had rematerialized into human form out of his own shadow. And now he was *inside* the house.

CHAPTER SEVEN

Ben found the sprig of blood rose under Jack's pillow. It was stiff and dry, but its cruel curved thorns were unmistakeable. Just one scratch would be fatal to a vampire.

He hurried back along the landing and reached the top of the stairs in time to see the shadow rematerialize inside the house. "Run!" Ben yelled.

Jack dived towards the stairs, dragging Henry after him. But Jerzy was lumbering after them, his arms outstretched, his dead fingers clawing the air.

"Did you find the blood rose?" Jack gasped. "We need it. Henry's Uncle Jerzy has come for a visit."

"I've got it," confirmed Ben, and he darted past Jack and Henry towards Jerzy. "Get back!" he shouted, and slashed at the vampire's arm with the sprig of blood rose.

The thorns scratched deep into Jerzy's flesh. One of them – the longest and sharpest – caught and snapped off, remaining hooked into Jerzy's skin. Jerzy let out a growl and hesitated. His pearly eyeballs seemed to roll deeper into their sockets and Ben felt a sudden flicker of hope. He'd done it! The blood rose had worked.

Weak with relief, Ben waited for the cracks to appear on Jerzy's skin, just as they had with all the other vampires he'd fought. In a moment Jerzy's flesh would split open, his insides would turn to gritty grey powder, and he would crumple into a pile of ash on the floor. . .

But nothing happened.

Jerzy stared at the long, cruel thorn sticking out of his arm. His breath rattled and hissed through his fangs. Then he simply plucked the rose-thorn out of his skin and threw it to the floor. The blood rose had had no effect on him at all!

"It's not working," Jack muttered, and the two boys exchanged a horrified look.

Ben knew exactly what his friend was thinking: a vampire who needed no invitation to enter a private residence, and who was immune to blood rose – how were they supposed to fight *this*?

Between them, Jack and Ben bundled Henry further up the stairs. The little boy stumbled, but recovered quickly and staggered upwards. Jack and Ben were right behind him. Ben half expected to feel Jerzy's hand clawing his shirt collar. In a moment, the vampire would seize hold of him, jerk him backwards and sink his fangs into Ben's throat. Ben could hear him growling.

Out of the corner of his eye, Ben saw a flicker of black on the red carpet. A shadow moved past him, sliding up the stairs as it moved. It pooled around Henry's feet, making the boy stop dead in his tracks. Then the shadow was past him. It grew into a solid shape, and suddenly Uncle Jerzy was there in front of them, in human form, his heavy body blocking their path.

Ben stared in horror. This creature could adopt some kind of shadow-form, like Camazotz's ability to shape-shift into a bat. But somehow so much worse. *You can fight a bat*, Ben thought. You could slash it with blood rose and bring it down. But how could you fight a shadow that had no physical form at all?

Henry staggered backwards. "Jack!" he gasped. "I thought you said them vampires had rules?"

"Looks like the rules have changed!" Jack replied grimly.

Without warning, Jerzy lunged at Henry. The expression on the vampire's face was greedy – almost *hungry* – Ben thought.

Jack shouted, "No!" and leapt forward to defend his friend, but Jerzy knocked him aside with a blow so strong that it sent Jack flying back down the stairs into Ben. Both boys crashed against the front door so hard that all the breath was knocked out of them.

On the stairs, Jerzy grabbed Henry by the wrist, jerked him close and sank his fangs into the boy's forearm.

Henry howled pitifully. Jack and Ben scrambled to

their feet and ran to help him. Ben was vaguely aware of Jack dragging Henry down the stairs to the hallway. Ben lunged up at Jerzy, but abruptly the creature vanished. It dissolved into shadow-form in the blink of an eye, and Ben found himself swiping at thin air. He twisted round just in time to see Jerzy's black shadow sliding away across the gold flock wallpaper.

Jack and Henry were over by the front door. Jack had torn back Henry's sleeve to inspect the younger boy's wound. Ben could see that there was no blood, just a circle of needle-sharp bite marks.

"He's been bitten," Ben muttered. "You know what that means, Jack?"

Jack turned to look at him, his eyes dark with dread. "Twice more, and he might become one of *them*."

"What?" Henry squealed in horror. "What are you talking about?"

"We've met vampires before," Ben explained grimly. "We found out that if they bite you three times, you turn into a vampire yourself. So whatever happens, Henry, don't get bitten again!"

"I – I'll try not to," Henry whispered, looking around fearfully for Uncle Jerzy.

The vampire's shadow slipped down the wall and pooled like tar on the hall carpet.

Face taut, Jack shoved Henry against the front door. "Stay behind me!" he said firmly.

Jack made a snatch at Jerzy's shadow, but the creature

danced away from him, flashing across the face of the grandfather clock. Then Jerzy rematerialized, his milky-white eyeballs glowing in the half-light. A guttural growl rattled in his throat.

Ben scrambled back to his feet and together the two boys lunged at Jerzy. Ben thought he had a grip and tried to hold on tight. But he realized almost immediately that he was clutching nothing but thin air. Jerzy had melted into shadow-form again. Then the creature was there, at the foot of the stairs, its feet planted wide on the plush carpet.

Ben could hear Henry sobbing with fear. Jack leapt forwards, and flung his arms around Jerzy's neck. But instantly the creature was vapour again, and Jack fell, tangled in his own thrashing arms. With Jack out of the way, Jerzy solidified again near the front door, looming over Henry's sobbing figure.

"No!" Henry pleaded.

Horrified, Ben clenched his fists together and clubbed Jerzy on the back of the head. Jerzy flinched, then simply changed to shadow again and slipped away. The creature rematerialized once more, but Ben felt relief to have actually landed a blow at all. It occurred to him that perhaps he'd only managed it because he'd caught Jerzy unawares.

To test his theory, Ben darted towards Jerzy. The creature was ready for him this time, and sure enough he swatted Ben away like a fly. The blow knocked the breath from Ben's body, so he could only watch in horror as Jerzy bent down close to Henry, sinking his teeth into Henry's shoulder, and making the boy turn white with pain.

"No!" Jack rushed forwards, reaching for Jerzy's shirt. Jerzy saw him, changed into shadow-form and slipped away beneath Jack's feet. No sooner had Jack turned to see where Jerzy had gone, than he was back again, sinking his fangs into Henry's leg.

"The third bite!" gasped Ben. He stared at Henry fearfully, his mind racing. Now, Henry would either die, or turn into a vampire himself. And then they were doomed, because how could he and Jack fight *two* of these strange new vampires?

But nothing happened. Henry continued to sob, sounding very human, as Jerzy sank his teeth into the little boy's flesh and gorged on his blood.

Ben and Jack gaped at each other. "This vampire definitely ain't the same as Camazotz's lot," Jack muttered.

"Well, you said the rules had changed," Ben pointed out, lunging at Jerzy and sending him flitting away in shadow-form.

"Yeah," Jack agreed. "But I didn't realize quite how much!" He shot Ben a meaningful look. "D'you reckon this is one of them lampirs?"

"Looks like it!" Ben replied.

But there was no time to talk, for Jerzy was back,

bending over Henry. He seemed able to drink blood from anywhere on the boy's body. Poor Henry struggled, gasping and kicking out. His foot caught Jerzy in the stomach and sent him spinning away in shadow-form. But the creature was back instantly, trying to fasten his gleaming fangs on to Henry's arm again.

"Over here! Try me!" Desperately, Ben tried to draw Jerzy away from Henry. He waved his arms and darted forwards into Jerzy's line of sight. But the vampire ignored him. His attention was all on Henry, his teeth biting down greedily on to the little boy's limbs – anywhere, everywhere. Henry wriggled and fought, but his struggles were getting weaker as he lost blood. With a sick feeling in the pit of his stomach, Ben realized that something had to be done – and fast – or they were going to lose this fight.

But what could they do? His mind raced. The only time they had scored any kind of hit on Jerzy was when he'd been taken by surprise – when Ben had managed to get behind him and club him on the back of the head. But fists hadn't really hurt him, so Ben knew he needed something more deadly. He must find a weapon and come up behind Jerzy while the vampire was distracted by Jack or Henry. And the more deadly the weapon, the more likely it was to end the fight once and for all.

Ben made a grab for Jack's arm. "Keep Jerzy busy for a minute. I've got an idea!" he muttered.

Jack nodded and leapt forwards with a yell, landing

a stinging blow on Jerzy's forehead. The creature disappeared into shadow-form and slid away up the wall.

Ben used the moment to hurry down the hallway. He shouldered through the door that led to the service areas of the house, making for the kitchens. The moonlight, slanting in through a barred window at the far end of the room, lit up a large wooden table. A dozen knives lay in a row at one end, their blades gleaming. *A dozen deadly weapons*, Ben thought grimly.

Without hesitation, Ben seized the largest knife and ran back to the hallway. Jerzy was in human-form, his back to Ben as he bore down on Henry who was cowering against the front door. Jack had thrown himself in front of Henry, his arms spread wide to protect the boy, who hid behind Jack's shoulder, his blood-stained arm flung up across his face as if he couldn't bear to see what was about to happen. Snarling, Jerzy bent forward, completely absorbed by the two boys.

Ben realized that this was the perfect moment to put his plan into action. Taking a deep breath, he gripped the knife tightly and hurled himself at Jerzy's back.

CHAPTER EIGHT

Before Ben could reach him, Jerzy let out a howl and turned angrily. He made a grab for Ben, fingers clawing at his arm, the gold signet ring glinting in the candlelight. But Ben twisted nimbly out of reach and the vampire's long black nails raked only air.

Ben watched the vampire move, carefully judging the best moment to strike. Then he slashed with the knife, just as Jerzy's hand swiped downwards. A terrible wail tore the air. The knife had sliced right through Jerzy's arm, just above the wrist!

Ben staggered backwards. Jerzy howled again and turned to shadow-form. His inky-black shape flickered away across the bottom of the stairs.

"Come on!" The knife still clutched in his fist, Ben dived forward and grabbed Henry, pulling him to his feet. Jack scrambled up too and all three boys made a dash for the drawing-room. The room was dark and full of shadows, the only light a dull orange glow from the dying fire. The Christmas tree in the corner glittered softly, its branches stretched out in front of the velvet curtains.

A low growl sounded behind them. Ben and Jack twisted round and stared in horror. Jerzy was following them! He loomed in the doorway, one moment in human-form, the next dissolving into shadow.

"Don't he ever give up?" Jack breathed.

"Seems not," Ben replied tightly. "But at least he's only got one hand now."

"I'd rather he only had one fang! How can we stop him?" Jack wondered, glancing about the room as if he was looking for a weapon.

Jerzy materialized right in front of them and lunged for Henry. Ben slashed at him with the knife again and the creature howled, melting away to shadow. Ben shoved Henry down behind an armchair. "Stay there," he said. "We'll deal with Jerzy, don't worry."

Jack, meanwhile, had made a dive for the fireplace, where the fire had now gone out. He crashed amongst the fire-irons for a moment, picking up brushes and shovels and tossing them aside. Then he found what he was looking for – a heavy iron poker. It was two feet long, with a gleaming brass handle and soot-blackened iron tip.

Swinging the poker left and right, Jack slashed at Jerzy. Jerzy growled and deflected the poker with his good arm. There was a dull thud as the poker whacked against his elbow, and the vampire made an angry sound.

As Ben watched his friend wield the poker, he noticed something strange. The vampire was no longer melting into shadow-form. With that realization Ben's hopes began to soar. A vampire in human-form – now that was something they could fight!

Jack gave a cry of triumph and stepped closer, clubbing Jerzy once . . . twice . . . three times! Each time Jerzy let out a howl of anguish and pain, but Jack didn't stop. He'd been in a few fights and knew exactly when to press home an advantage.

But across the room, in the dark grate, a heap of coal embers collapsed and sent showers of sparks up the chimney. Jerzy lumbered forward into the glowing light – and slipped into shadow-form. The light from the embers died and Ben lost sight of Jack and Jerzy in the darkness. But he assumed the creature must have resumed physical form, because he heard Jack's poker connect and the creature give a grunt of pain.

Ben's thoughts raced. The creature seemed to be having trouble using his shadow-form to escape here in the drawing-room, but *why*? Ben glanced around the room, trying to see what was different. And then it hit him – the room was too dark! The curtains were drawn, shutting out the moonlight and even the dull glow from the fire had now died. Where there was no light, Jerzy couldn't have a shadow.

But there was still some light – just a sliver – filtering

in from the hall through the half-open drawing-room door –

Ben hurled himself across the room and slammed the door shut. Instantly the drawing-room was plunged into total darkness.

"What'd you do that for?" Jack exclaimed sharply. "I can't see a bleedin' thing!"

"Sorry," Ben groped his way across the room towards Jack in the dark. "But if there's no light, then you can't have a shadow. And if you can't have a shadow, then you can't slip into shadow-form . . . understand?"

"Oh yes," Jack replied in a grim voice. "I understand all right. But how do we fight him –" there was a swishing sound as Jack's poker sliced the air again – "in the bleedin' dark?"

"We listen," Ben said simply.

Henry whimpered from behind the armchair.

"Sssh. . ." Jack hissed.

There was silence.

Shoulder-to-shoulder, Ben and Jack circled warily, listening hard for any sound that might tell them where Jerzy was.

But there was nothing. Just deep, dark silence, and a hammering pulse that filled Ben's ears. Then another sound broke through. A scratching, creaking sound outside the drawing-room door. . .

"Oh, blimey," Jack breathed. "Don't tell me there's more of 'em!"

The scratching sound grew louder as the door swung open. It was Emily, and she had an oil lamp in her hand.

Bright white light filled the room, and Jack yelled, "No!"

CHAPTER NINE

Emily had been drifting into a troubled sleep when she heard a door being slammed somewhere downstairs. Instantly she was awake, sitting bolt upright and staring into the shadows of her bedroom. Her gauze curtains rippled, ghostly in the half-light, and she listened for more sound. Then she heard a muffled thump, as if someone had bumped into a chair.

Puzzled, Emily decided to go and see what the commotion was. There was a tall, slender oil lamp on her nightstand. Taking only a moment to light it, she turned the wick down low so that there was just enough flame to see by. She carried the lamp in one hand and made her way down the stairs, listening hard. There was something going on in the drawing-room – she was sure of it. She turned the door handle and pushed the door wide.

The white light from the oil lamp set the room aglow. She could make out the Christmas tree in the corner, its decorations twinkling. And there was *Henry* cowering by an armchair, his face deathly pale and his shirt and coat all torn.

She didn't have time to notice anything else, because someone – she thought it was Jack – shouted, "No!" and abruptly a figure lumbered out of the darkness towards her. Emily caught a glimpse of a man's distorted face, his eyeballs white and opaque, his lips peeled back to reveal a mouth full of fangs. Then the figure rippled and shimmered – and vanished!

Emily sensed something over her shoulder and whirled just in time to see the creature reappear behind her. He seemed to have rematerialized out of his own shadow, and Emily felt horror sweep through her as he lunged, reaching for her with a claw-like hand. Not knowing what to do, Emily hurled the oil lamp at the man, hoping to stop the creature in his tracks.

He batted the lamp away, sending it crashing to the floor, but lamp-oil splashed up on to his trousers. A vivid blue flame skittered across the surface of the rug as the hot wick touched the oil. Emily just had time to twist away and fling up an arm to protect her face before the lamp-oil on the creature's trousers ignited and it burst into flames.

He burned furiously, rearing and twisting, agony etched across his features. The skin across his cheekbones shrivelled. The claw-like hands flared and crisped. There was a terrible stench in the air, of lamp-oil and seared flesh. In seconds, the creature had burned to ash and cinders. For a moment the body held its shape, then it collapsed in on itself.

And abruptly there was nothing. Just a pile of ash heaped on the rug.

"Emily! Are you all right?" Ben dashed across the room to his sister. Jack was right behind him. Together they stamped out the few tiny flames that still flickered on the carpet.

"Yes," Emily said in bewilderment. "I'm all right. But what was that? What on earth have I done?"

"You done what we been trying to do for about half an hour," Jack replied, as Ben quietly closed the drawing-room door. "You've just killed a vampire, or a lampir – a monster, anyway!"

Emily stared at him in horror. "A vampire? Here in this house?"

"In this very room," Ben confirmed grimly, as he lit a candle. The flickering flame chased the shadows into the corners of the room.

"He used to be Henry's Uncle Jerzy," Jack explained. "Henry was right. Somebody *was* following him."

Henry crawled out from behind the armchair and rubbed his cuff under his nose. "Jerzy was hiding in the gardens across the road," he said in a small voice. "He came right up to the house. But Jack wouldn't let him in. He told him to go away."

"But I couldn't stop him entering the house, Emily."

Jack shook his head as if he couldn't believe what had happened. "He just came in – without an invitation. And look!" Jack showed Emily all Henry's bite marks. "He's been bitten more than three times, but he hasn't changed into a vampire himself."

"Thank goodness," Ben put in. "We had enough trouble fighting just one of them. It was immune to blood rose, Em. . ."

Emily gaped. "Blood rose? Where did you get that from?"

"I had some under me pillow," Jack said sheepishly. "Brought it back from Mexico, just in case. Not that it made a blind bit of difference. Might as well have been a sprig of holly for all the damage it did to Jerzy." He frowned and glanced down at the heap of Jerzy's ashes. "This creature's a bit different to the vampires we're used to dealing with, Emily. Reckon it must be one of those lampirs."

Ben nodded. "It's *very* different," he agreed. "And very powerful. It can take on a kind of shadow-form, Em. And it had many more fangs than Camazotz's vampires! It seemed to be able to drink blood from anywhere on Henry's body."

Jack shuddered. "I thought Henry was a goner at one point. Good job you went for the knife when you did."

"*Knife?*" Emily echoed, growing more amazed and horrified by the moment.

"From the kitchen," Ben explained. "And I'd better put it back there before Cook notices."

Before he could move, however, the drawing-room door flew open and Mrs Mills appeared. In spite of her tartan dressing-gown and the frilly bonnet she wore over her curls at night, she was a force to be reckoned with. She bristled in the doorway, arms folded.

"What, may I ask, is going on here?" Her gaze swept across the boys in their outdoor clothes, and the heap of ash on the carpet. "It's gone midnight and I was under the impression you were all in bed! But here you are, in the drawing-room, with the carpet burnt almost to a cinder." She stomped across to Jerzy's ashes and poked at them with the toe of her slipper. "This rug is ruined. What on earth have you been doing in here?"

Jack hurried to explain. "The fire can't have been out properly. Some embers must have spilled on to the carpet and set it alight." He still had the poker in his hand, and Emily thought he looked quite convincing as he pointed it in the direction of the fireplace. "Luckily we caught it in time."

"We'll clean it up," Ben put in. "Don't worry."

"Worry? I'm not *worried*, Master Benedict." The frilly edges of Mrs Mills's bonnet quivered with indignation. "I am extremely disappointed in Tillet, that's what I am! She's responsible for damping down the fires last thing at night. The careless girl might have burnt the house down!"

"Oh. . ." Jack looked horrified at having got Tillet into

trouble. "No! It wasn't Tillet's fault. It was me. I—"

But Mrs Mills's alert gaze had settled on Henry. "And who, may I ask, is *this*?"

Ben quickly put an arm around Henry's thin shoulders. "This is our friend Henry," he said. "He's going to stay with us tonight."

"Is he indeed?" Mrs Mills frowned, looking Henry up and down. She took in his tear-stained face and grubby, torn clothes.

Henry gazed solemnly back at her, his expression pitiful. "If it's no trouble, missus," he said softly.

Mrs Mills propped her hands on her hips and shook her head in despair. But her mouth twitched into a smile as she said, "I'll make one condition, Master Benedict. If your young friend is going to sleep in my nice clean sheets, then he must have a bath first!"

"Bath!" A look of horror passed over Henry's face. "I ain't 'avin' no bath!"

Jack grinned. "After the kind of day you've had, Henry, I should think a bath is the least of your worries. Come on!"

Mrs Mills shooed Jack and Henry out of the drawing-room. Emily and Ben could hear her chattering away as she bustled them upstairs, "Pyjamas . . . and a vest . . . and a bar of carbolic soap. . ." All thoughts of blaming Tillet for anything had obviously been forgotten.

Ben grinned as he started to clear up. "Poor Henry," he said.

CHAPTER TEN

"There we go, Master Jack," Mrs Mills said briskly. "Your young friend Henry should be cosy enough there on the sofa once he's out of the bath. I've given him a goosedown quilt and three woollen blankets." She shook her head and tutted softly. "Poor little mite hasn't got a scrap of fat on his bones to keep him warm. We shall have to see about feeding him up, won't we?"

When Mrs Mills had gone, Jack threw himself down on his bed and stared at the ceiling for a moment. What a night! He thought back to the early evening, when he'd been standing in front of the fireplace in the drawing-room waiting for Ben and Emily to come back from the Royal Institution. He'd been pondering his nice new life, thinking about spending his first Christmas as a gentleman. . .

But gentlemen, Jack told himself with a grin, *do not generally go running about in moonlit graveyards. Nor do they fight ferocious battles with the living dead!* He patted his jacket pocket, slipped his hand in and drew out the sprig of blood rose. He'd found it just now, sticking up out of the carpet in the hallway. Mrs Mills had almost trodden on it as she took Henry by the hand and led him upstairs.

Jack twirled the broken stem thoughtfully between finger and thumb. He didn't know why he'd picked it up, really. Blood rose had been a vital weapon in their fight against Camazotz's servants, yet it had proved useless against Uncle Jerzy. Jack really hoped that Jerzy was the only lampir around, because if there were any more, how on earth were he, Ben and Emily going to fight them? They couldn't chase them all with oil lamps. . .

A wave of tiredness fogged Jack's brain. He couldn't think about this now, it would be much better to talk it over with the others in the morning. He rubbed his eyes and stared blearily at the bedroom door. Where was Henry? The little lad had been in the bathroom a long time. Maybe he'd got lost – Jack remembered how enormous the house had seemed to him when he first arrived.

He got up and padded down the hallway towards the bathroom. He paused at the top of the stairs. Moonlight slanted in through the window at the far end of the landing, lighting up a bowl of orchids which stood on a small, semi-circular table against the wall. But there wasn't any sign of Henry.

Worry gnawed at Jack, so he went all the way along to

the bathroom and tapped on the door. "Henry?" he whispered.

There was no answer.

Jack knocked again, louder this time. From inside the room he heard a hollow thud, as if something heavy had hit the wooden floorboards.

Icy fear rippled down Jack's spine. "Henry?" he cried urgently. "Henry, are you all right?"

There was still no answer, so Jack opened the bathroom door.

There was Henry – stretched on the floor beside the claw-footed iron bath, half-dressed in a pair of Ben's pyjama bottoms and a white vest. Tooth-marks from Jerzy's fangs still showed on his arms and legs, dark-red against his pale skin. But that wasn't all; Henry's face was bright red and his eyes bulged. He gasped for breath and kicked out with both feet, heels scraping uselessly against the slippery floorboards.

Shocked, Jack dashed forwards into the room and dropped to his knees beside the younger boy. "Henry, what are you *doing*?" he cried.

But no sooner were the words out of his mouth than he saw exactly what Henry was doing. He was struggling to prize blackened fingers away from his neck where they threatened to choke the life out of him. He was fighting with his Uncle Jerzy's severed hand!

CHAPTER ELEVEN

Jack wrenched the hand away from Henry's throat. It felt as if it was alive – writhing and pulsing. He wrestled with it for a moment, trying to get a grip on the cold flesh. But the muscular fingers flexed and tightened so quickly that Jack couldn't keep hold.

"Hang on to it, Jack!" Henry begged him, scrambling away across the floor. "Don't let it get me again!"

"I'm . . . trying. . ." Jack gasped. He gritted his teeth with the effort and felt sweat break out on his forehead as he fought the hand. It jerked and writhed, reaching for Jack's throat.

The hand gave a powerful jerk away from Jack and finally he let go. He made a last despairing grab at the hand as it fell, but it hit the floor and scuttled away like a huge spider. The signet ring on the middle finger gleamed like a single eye as it headed for the door. Jack chased after it, racing along the landing.

He could see the hand, just ahead of him. It reached

the top of the stairs, reared up on the stump of its wrist, and leapt down the steps, making a horrible, heavy bumping sound as it hit each tread.

Jack dashed after the hand, his own feet pounding down the stairs. He took the last two steps at a leap, landing heavily on the hallway carpet. He narrowly missed crashing into the gong and waking up the whole house.

The hand scuttled sideways away from him. It reached the mottled pool of light that slanted in through the stained glass panels of the door, and melted into shadow-form.

Jack caught up with it just as it pooled like black ink, rippled sideways and disappeared under the front door.

"Good riddance!" Jack muttered. He waited at the door for what felt like an eternity to see whether it would come back.

But the hand didn't come back and Jack was finally satisfied that it had gone. As a precaution, he nudged the doormat with his foot, pushing it up against the crack under the door. Then he trudged back up the stairs, feeling suddenly exhausted. It felt as though this day was never going to end! He'd been up since dawn, brushing down his black suit ready for Molly's funeral. Then he'd made the journey across London, not once but twice. Then he'd fought a shadow-shifting vampire, *and* its hand!

Henry was still in the bathroom, perched on the edge

of the bath. He was trembling from head to foot and taking in great gulps of air. One hand was pressed to his throat as if he could still feel the hand throttling him.

"You all right?" Concerned for his friend, Jack sat on the edge of the bath next to Henry. "Let me have a look at your neck. . . Hmmm, it doesn't look too bad. A bit of bruising, but that'll fade in a day or two. Lucky those horrible black nails didn't scratch you. Here, put on your pyjama jacket. Reckon you're shaking as much from the cold as anything."

Henry swallowed painfully and began to button up his pyjamas. "Why did Uncle Jerzy want to kill me, Jack?" he asked. "When he was alive, he took care of me. We didn't have no money or nothing, but Jerzy always made sure I had the juiciest bits of meat from the stew pot. When I was younger, he built a little bed from packing crates he'd begged from the docks." Henry's eyes clouded with tears as he remembered all the things that Jerzy had done for him in life. "Uncle Jerzy used to love me. So why did he want to kill me? It don't make sense, Jack."

Jack sighed and shook his head. "What you have to understand is that it weren't really Uncle Jerzy that was trying to kill you."

"It looked like Uncle Jerzy," Henry said in a trembling voice.

Jack shook his head. "Uncle Jerzy's dead. That

78

creature was just using Jerzy's shell, his body, to walk about and do 'orrible things."

Henry shuddered and Jack gave him a reassuring pat on the back. "The important thing is, he's gone now. And it's about time we got some sleep."

Henry was still pale, but he looked calmer when Jack tucked the goosedown quilt around him a few minutes later. And by the time Jack blew out the candle and climbed into his own bed, he knew that the younger boy was asleep.

Jack lay back on his pillows with his hands folded behind his head, staring at the ceiling as he listened to Henry's regular breathing.

It was at least an hour before he himself slipped into a dreamless sleep.

CHAPTER TWELVE

Pale winter sunlight slanted in through the dining-room window, lighting up the crisp white tablecloth and making the silver knives and forks glitter.

"What a beautiful morning!" exclaimed one of the maids, Evans, as she breezed in through the swing-doors. Her face was hidden behind an enormous silver tray laden with tea cups and little china pots, but Emily knew that Evans would have rosy cheeks and a wide smile. Evans was always smiling, and her cheeks were always rosy because she spent so much time outside in the cold. She was "courting", as Mrs Mills put it. This meant that Evans spent an awful lot of time chatting to the handsome young man who delivered eggs and milk to all the houses in Bedford Square.

"Morning, Evans," Ben said as the maid placed one of the little china pots on his breakfast plate. The back of her hand brushed his and he grinned. "Gracious me, your fingers are cold. Have you been outside?" Ben checked his pocket-watch, which said that the time was just gone nine o'clock. "So early? And on such a chilly morning?"

Evans blushed so that her cheeks turned from rose-pink to brick-red. "W-well, M-master Benedict. . ." she stammered.

"Ignore him, Evans," Emily said with a smile. "He's teasing you!"

"Oh!" Evans flapped her hand at Ben. "You're a devil, you are." But her face was all smiles as she went round with the teapot.

Everybody began to eat breakfast. Jack dived for the toast. Ben stabbed his knife into the butter dish. Emily picked up her egg spoon. But Henry did nothing. He was sitting across the table from Emily, wearing a white shirt of Ben's with his hair neatly parted and brushed. A small linen bandage on his arm covered bites from Jerzy's fangs. He looked very serious, and watched Jack carefully as though he wasn't quite sure what to do with the little china pot that Evans had placed before him.

Jack lifted the lid of his pot. There was a poached egg inside, and Jack dug in enthusiastically. Henry carefully copied him, and Emily saw his serious expression melt away in a grin as he tucked into his egg.

Jack finished first. He leant across the table and told Ben and Emily all about his fight with Jerzy's severed hand, while they finished their food.

The Coles listened to Jack's grim tale in silence. Then Ben pushed his plate away and sighed.

"You know," he said thoughtfully, "we're going to have to find that man who burst into Sir Peter's lecture yesterday. He may have the answers to a lot of our questions."

Emily nodded. "I've been thinking the same thing," she said. "It seems he wasn't as mad as he appeared." She turned to Jack. "You thought he was Polish, didn't you?"

Jack nodded. "Sounded like it."

"There's a Polish connection to this whole business," Ben pointed out. "Sir Peter went on an expedition to Poland. The myth of the Dhampir Bell is all about a plague that killed a lot of people in Poland. And Henry's Uncle Jerzy was Polish—"

"And that's not all," Emily cut in eagerly. "Jack, didn't you tell us once that Molly was originally from Poland?"

Jack nodded. "She was," he said, idly twisting Molly's ring round on his finger. "And I've been thinking about her running out in front of that wagon the night she died. Molly was a brave sort, not someone who'd be easily spooked. It seems to me she might have been running from one of these lampirs."

"I'd certainly run from one," Emily said with a shudder. "Like the wind!"

"So, where shall we start our search for this Polish fellow?" Ben asked.

Jack looked thoughtful. "The cemetery?" he suggested.

"We could ask around – see if anybody remembers him."

"Good idea," Ben agreed.

Emily smiled across the table at Henry and said, "What about you, Henry? Would you like to come with us?"

But Henry shook his head firmly. "I want to get back to me usual haunts down the dockside," he said with a bashful smile. "Catch up with me old friends. And now that you've got rid of that . . . that *creature* . . . well, I feel safe again!"

"Creature? What creature?" Mrs Mills asked as she came in with Evans who was carrying another enormous tray.

The friends glanced at each other in alarm. "Nothing!" they chorused quickly.

However, Mrs Mills didn't look convinced. "I distinctly heard Henry say 'creature'," she said. "What creature? Is there something in the house?"

"Not a *creature*, Mrs Mills," Ben said, his eyes widening as he thought fast. "Henry said *teacher*. . . Yes, that's it, teacher. We were just talking about Jack learning to read. And Henry said that Emily must be a really good *teacher*. . ."

Mrs Mills beamed warmly, first at Emily and then at Jack. "A good teacher," she agreed. "And a very good pupil! Now, what are your plans for the day?"

Emily thought quickly. She knew they couldn't tell

Mrs Mills the whole truth, because that would mean admitting that there really had been a "creature". But she didn't like to lie. "We thought we'd see Henry safely home," she said finally. It had occurred to her that if Henry wanted to go back to the dockside, then they could drop him off and still be quite near to the cemetery. "We'll take him in a hansom, and save him the walk. . ."

"To Tooley Street!" Henry put in cheerfully, and Emily shot him a grateful smile.

"*Tooley Street?*" Mrs Mills raised an eyebrow. "Why, that's south of the river! I quite agree, Miss Emily. Henry can't walk all that way. A hansom cab is a fine idea. I'll send Evans out to call one."

The hansom cab was duly summoned, and the four friends crammed themselves on to its narrow seat. The driver flicked the reins and the cab set off at a brisk pace, only slowing down when they came to the congested traffic of Cheapside. Cutting the city neatly in half from west to east, Cheapside was said to be the busiest thoroughfare in London, if not the world. And it was easy to see why, Emily thought. Dozens of streets and lanes criss-crossed it, in all directions. A mass of pedestrians, wagons, carriages and cabs all jostled for room. Eager apprentices stood in shop doorways bawling for trade. Their cries echoed up to the rooftops: "What d'ye lack?" and "Finest linen here!"

At last they left Cheapside behind and the hansom

was able to speed up, bowling briskly over London Bridge and down into Tooley Street, where the cab drew in to the side of the road. Ben paid the driver, and the friends found themselves deposited in the midst of the hurly-burly docks.

A nearby pie shop was doing brisk business, and the heavenly fragrance of hot pastry mingled with the smell of ships' tar and riverweed. Sailors in blue stood in a line waiting to buy pies, whistling cheery tunes and jingling their pennies in their cupped hands. Across the road some shabby children played hopscotch, dodging the piles of horse dung. A constant stream of loaded wagons lumbered past, bearing goods to and from the huge warehouses that crowded the riverside.

The friends stood awkwardly for a moment, all of them looking at Henry. He gazed back at them, his pinched little face solemn.

At last Emily broke the silence. She gave Henry a hug, then unwrapped her red woollen scarf from around her neck and tucked it around his. "Here," she said. "I want to give you this. It'll keep you warm."

Henry snuggled the scarf up under his chin. "Thanks, Emily," he said shyly.

Ben and Jack both shook hands with the little lad. "Remember," Jack told him, "if there's anything you need, you come and find me. All right?"

"All right, then." Henry grinned. "I'll be seeing yer. . ." And he was gone, slipping into the crowd with the ease of someone who was back on their own territory. Emily caught a flash of red – her scarf – but then Henry had vanished.

Ben touched her elbow. "Come on," he said gently. "We've got work to do. Remember?"

The cemetery looked different in the daytime, no longer eerie and full of shadows. The huge wrought-iron gates stood open, and when Emily glanced in she thought that the graveyard resembled nothing more sinister than a big garden full of stone statues. Obviously other people thought the same, because there were several couples strolling arm in arm along the gravel pathways, and a boy playing with a little dog.

Jack came to a halt just inside the gates. "It was here that I saw him," he said. "There was a crowd of about ten people. And our Polski bloke was shouting and stirring them up with his talk of dead bodies and all." Jack looked suddenly grim. "Wish I'd paid a bit more attention to what he was saying, now."

"You weren't to know," Emily pointed out. She turned a full circle, gazing around the cemetery. "Well, it's obvious he's not here now. I think we should split up and ask around. Let's start talking to people. Find out whether they were here yesterday and ask if they remember seeing him."

Half an hour later the friends met back at the cemetery gates. Each of them had talked to a dozen different people, but nobody remembered seeing a little Polish man with wild hair.

Ben sighed. "What do we do now?"

Jack narrowed his eyes, watching a lad of about Henry's age who was walking up and down in front of the cemetery gates. The boy was dressed in brown breeches and a threadbare jacket. Strung across his chest was a huge cloth bag crammed with newspapers.

"*London Gazette!*" the boy cried. "Mining Disaster in Wales. . . Latest! Thirteen dead."

"Wait here a moment," Jack said. "I've got an idea."

He felt in his pocket for some money and approached the newspaper boy. "Hello, mate," he said, flashing the lad a friendly smile. "I'm looking for a bloke I saw hanging round here yesterday. . . Small bloke with wild hair. Stirring up the crowd something rotten, he was. . ."

The newspaper boy grinned. "You mean Filip Cinska?" he said. He pronounced it "Chinska", like chin or chimney. "Polish bloke. Wears a dusty old tailcoat and stripy trousers."

Jack nodded, jingling a couple of coins in the palm of his hand. "And d'you happen to know where this Filip Cinska lives?" he asked.

The lad eyed the coins. "Not sure as I remember too well. Give us what you've got in yer 'and and it might come back to me. . ."

Jack rolled his eyes. "Think I was born yesterday? You

tells me what I want to know and *then* I gives you the money."

The lad winked at Jack. "No flies on you, is there? All right, guv, I'll tell yer. Filip Cinska's got lodgings at Widow Kaminski's place – above the watch and clock shop in Tiler's Alley."

Jack grinned. "Thank you," he said, and flipped the boy a couple of coins.

Tiler's Alley was a narrow lane off Tooley Street, full of crooked little houses and tiny shops with bow windows. The friends found the watch and clock shop easily. There was a small sign on the door next to it which said: *Paulina Kaminski – rooms weekly or monthly*.

Widow Kaminski turned out to be a hunched, wizened old lady dressed in a dusty black gown and a grey linen bonnet. She had a plug of chewing tobacco tucked into her cheek, and it had turned her stumpy teeth bright yellow. "Attic," she said curtly, when Ben asked for Filip Cinska, and jerked her thumb over her shoulder.

Eyes narrowed, she turned and watched as the three friends trooped up the winding wooden staircase. "No noise, mind!" she called after them. "I don't like a rowdy house."

The wooden stairs went up and around, up and around, zigzagging through the middle of the tall house until Emily thought they might come out on the rooftops. The stairwell was dark and dusty, and smelled of mouse-droppings, but finally the three friends reached the top. They found themselves on a tiny landing, next to a door set into the chipped and peeling wall.

"I suppose this is it," Ben said, slightly breathless from the climb. "Who's going to knock?"

"I will," Emily volunteered bravely. She stepped forwards and rapped hard on the door.

There was a scuffling sound, then the door flew open and Filip Cinska stood there in his dusty old tailcoat and striped trousers. He looked exactly as he had at the lecture the previous evening – with the same wild blond hair and intense blue eyes. He obviously hadn't shaved, judging by the bristling blond stubble on his jaw. Buttons were missing from the front of his jacket and there was a smear of blood on his frayed cuff. Jack wondered if the bloke normally looked this scruffy, or whether the missing buttons and the blood were the result of his scuffle with the guards at the Royal Institution that Ben and Emily had described.

Filip Cinska stared blankly at Emily and Ben for a moment, then his tired gaze settled on Jack. Instantly his expression brightened. He stepped forwards, grasped Jack's hand, and began to shake it vigorously. A huge smile lit up his face. *"Co jest wasze imie nazwa?"* he cried, gazing at Jack as if he was an old friend.

Jack looked confused. "Sorry, mate, I don't speak Polish," he responded. He shot a look at Ben and Emily. "None of us do."

"No? Are you sure?" Filip Cinska's smile faded a little. "What is your name?"

"I'm Jack Harkett. And these are my friends, Emily and Benedict Cole. We've come to see you about—"

But Filip Cinska shook his head. "Wait! First I want to know where you are from, Mister Jack Harkett."

"From round here," Jack replied warily.

The little man's smile disappeared, to be replaced with a look of disappointment. "What about your parents?" he asked quietly.

"Me parents?" Jack shrugged. "I never knew 'em, so your guess is as good as mine."

Filip Cinska brightened again. "So you are an orphan, Mister Harkett? Then maybe your parents were Polish. . . ?"

Jack shook his head. "Nah, far as I know, they were English an' I'm English."

"You are sure of this?"

"Sure as I can be," Jack said. "Why?"

Cinska looked as if he was going to say something else, but then he shook his head. "No matter. . ." Turning to Emily he said cheerfully, "I am charmed to meet you, Emily Cole." He gave a very formal bow and said in his curious, heavily-accented English, "How can I be of service to you?"

"Well, Mister Cinska," Emily began. She glanced at Jack and Ben and saw them both nod in encouragement. "We want to talk to you about lampirs."

All Filip Cinska's good humour drained away. His face turned deathly white and for one horrible moment Emily thought he was going to faint.

But he didn't. Instead, he pushed the door to his attic room wide open and said quietly, "I think you had better come in."

CHAPTER THIRTEEN

"Sit down, my friends." Filip Cinska dusted off the only chair with the sleeve of his coat, and gestured for Emily to sit on it. Then he pulled a selection of rickety wooden stools from under an equally rickety table and waved Jack and Ben on to them. "Yes. . . Please. . . Sit down and be comfortable!"

Jack waited until Ben and Emily were settled on one side of the table, then perched on a stool next to Filip Cinska. The little Polish man was still staring at him, and Jack had no idea why the bloke was so convinced he knew him. Jack wondered guiltily if he had picked Cinska's pocket at some time in the past. It was possible. He'd picked a lot of pockets in this very alley. Not because he'd wanted to, but because it was the only way for a boy like him to avoid starvation. You had to do what you had to do. . .

Jack wondered how long Filip Cinska had been living in Tiler's Alley, but a quick glance around the room gave him no clues. The little attic was sparsely furnished, with a sloping ceiling and a single, grimy window that looked out across the crooked rooftops of London. In one corner stood a pot-bellied stove with a blackened chimney, which gave off a comforting warmth. Beside the stove, another door led through to a small bedroom. Jack could just make out a sagging bed covered in a multi-coloured patchwork quilt.

"So you want to talk to me about lampirs?" Filip Cinska prompted. He looked from Emily, who was unbuttoning her coat and pulling off her gloves, to Ben and then Jack. "What do three English children know about lampirs?"

All three of the friends hesitated. Then Emily said cautiously, "Actually, Mr Cinska, we think we've seen one."

At this, Filip Cinska tore his gaze away from Jack and stared at Emily. "You haf seen a lampir?" His voice dropped to a whisper. "Here . . . in London?"

Emily nodded and glanced at Jack. "Tell him about last night, Jack," she urged.

Cinska looked at Jack too, his eyes an intense bright blue. "Yes, please," he said. "It is important that you tell me *exactly* what you haf seen."

"Well, we was in the cemetery off Tooley Street, just before midnight," Jack began. "I'd been there earlier, see – for a funeral – and I dropped a ring that was really precious to me." He showed Cinska Molly's ring, glinting on his middle finger. "I wanted to go back for it, so Ben and Emily said they'd come with me. We was worried about grave-robbers. But as it turned out, grave-robbers was the last thing we should have been bothered about!"

Filip Cinska listened intently as Jack recounted the events of the previous evening – the creature clawing its way out of the grave in the moonlight, Henry thinking he was being followed, the fight with Uncle Jerzy.

"You fought with it?" The little Polish man's blue eyes were so wide that Jack thought they might pop out of his head. "You actually *fought* with a lampir?"

Jack nodded. "As best we could. It was so strong – stronger than a man."

Cinska nodded. "Yes. A lampir has ze strength of ten men." He looked first at Jack and then across the table to Ben, his expression full of admiration. "You were both very brave. And did it use shadow-form?"

Jack nodded, trying to swallow the sense of horror that the memory gave him.

"I wanted to ask you about the shadows," Ben put in. "How does a lampir do that?"

Cinska spread his hands wide and shrugged. "I do not know ze *how*, Benedict Cole. But I can tell you that shadow-form is one of ze lampir's best forms of defence. At night, where there is moonlight, or some artificial light – say, candlelight or a gas lamp – then ze creature has ze ability to adopt shadow-form and dart away from danger."

"Moonlight, candlelight or gas lamps?" Emily said with a frown. "What about sunlight? *Daylight?*"

Cinska shook his head. "Daylight is ze enemy of ze lampir. It *forces* ze lampir into shadow-form, and keeps him there until darkness falls. A lampir cannot take his physical form when there is daylight." He looked at Ben and Jack again, studying them closely with a small frown between his brows. "But you boys haf lived to tell ze tale, so am I correct in guessing that you defeated ze creature?"

Jack swallowed hard. "We killed him or rather, Emily did," he explained. "Ben and I tried, but the lampir was too strong."

"We tried everything we could think of," Ben put in. "I even stabbed Jerzy with a knife, and cut off his hand. But that had a mind of its own. It ran off and hid – tried to attack Henry later. It's gone now," he added hastily, seeing Cinska's horrified expression. "Then Emily came downstairs with an oil lamp. She threw it at Jerzy and it set fire to him."

"Fire!" Cinska leaned eagerly across the table towards Emily. "You set fire to ze lampir – and at the end it was nothing but grey ash, yes?"

Emily nodded, and the little Polish man sat back again, clearly relieved. "That is good. Lampirs, they are very afraid of fire – and rightly so. It is one of ze few weapons we haf in our fight against them. If you burned him, this Jerzy, then he is truly dead."

For a moment Filip Cinska was silent. Then he sighed. "I am afraid that although you three have destroyed Jerzy, this is only ze beginning. There will be others. I haf seen ze signs."

The friends exchanged worried looks. "Signs of what?" Jack asked.

Filip Cinska took a long, deep breath. "Alas, for you to understand fully, my friends, I must go back to ze beginning. It is a long story."

Jack glanced at Ben and Emily. "We've got all day, Mister Cinska."

"Call me Filip, please." He waved away the "Mister" with one thin hand. "All right, if you want to hear ze story, then I will tell you. But first, I am ze host, no? I must make tea for my friends!" He bustled over to the pot-bellied stove and cranked open the door. There flames flared as he stirred the coals with an iron poker. He tossed in some more fuel, then set a rusty old kettle on the top of the stove to boil.

At last he began his story. . .

"Many, many years ago in Poland," Filip said, reaching up to a narrow wooden shelf above the stove, "there was a plague."

He took a tin down from the shelf, prised the lid off, and then emptied what looked like shredded tree-bark into a teapot. "This plague was so terrible," he explained, "that its story has been passed down through ze generations, ever since. It was an illness that our

Polish ancestors had never encountered before. Those who caught it were ill for a period of exactly twenty-one days – and then they died. Our ancestors buried them, as usual, in ze graveyards and mourned them. But something had changed, because death was somehow not death, no! For when ze moon was visible in ze night sky, and moonlight struck ze earth, those dead bodies climbed out of their graves and began to walk!"

Jack caught Ben's eye and knew exactly what his friend was thinking. There had been a moon last night. . .

Filip lifted four tea-glasses down from the shelf. They were made from smoke-coloured glass set in two-handled silver holders. "These dead came looking for their living relatives," he continued. "At first nobody knew why they came. But soon it became very clear. The walking dead were hungry – hungry for ze blood of their families. They had grown teeth, you see – great fangs which pierced ze skin and allowed ze lampirs to drink, and drink, and drink."

Something which had bothered Jack the previous evening suddenly made sense to him now. "So that's why Jerzy didn't bother to bite Ben and me," he said. "Jerzy only wanted Henry's blood, because lampirs can only drink the blood of their own relatives."

"I noticed that too," Ben said eagerly. "And I remember Sir Peter saying at the lecture that the dead killed their relatives. Does that mean that a lampir is only a danger to his own family?"

Cinska lined up the tea-glasses on the table. "I'm afraid, Benedict, that that is only ze case for a short time. It is true that when they are newly-risen from their graves, lampirs can drink only ze blood of people related to them. This blood is closely matched to their own. It gives them their life and their superhuman strength. But later," Filip grimaced, "later, they may drink *any* blood. It is at this point that they become vicious hunters, seeking the blood of any living human – man, woman, or child."

"I see." Ben swallowed hard. "So you're saying that, in time, we could all become victims."

"I am afraid so," Cinska murmured. "And things are much worse than I thought. You see, I haf seen ze signs."

"The signs?" Emily prompted, glancing at Ben and Jack. "What signs have you seen, Filip?"

The Polish man folded his arms across his thin chest. "Ze first marker of ze plague is a strange purple colouring of ze fingernails. . ." he said slowly.

Jack glanced quickly down at his own hands, and noticed that Ben and Emily were doing the same.

Ben caught Jack's eye and grimaced. "The hansom cab driver," he whispered. "His nails were purple last night. . ."

Filip Cinska went on, "Ze next symptom is a feeling of great cold which takes over your whole body, as though a tide of ice is sweeping through your veins. And then you feel tired, as if your bones are made of lead. You must give in to gravity and lie down. Lie down anywhere! In Poland I haf seen people stretched out on ze roadside, on doorsteps, in fields where they were working. Once they lie down it is ze end, for they will not rise again until after death."

"Is it very catching?" Ben asked, and Jack knew that he was thinking of the hansom driver. The three friends had sat beneath him in the cab as he'd driven them halfway across London last night. He'd breathed all over them. . .

But thankfully, Filip was shaking his head. "It is infectious, but you must haf close contact with an infected person to catch ze sickness yourself."

Ben looked relieved. In the background, the kettle began to make a shrill, shrieking noise, and Cinska hurried to lift it off the stove. "We still do not know exactly how ze plague is passed from person to person," he explained as he filled the teapot with hot water. "But my brother, Roman, he is a scientist. How do you say, *doktor*?"

"Yes, a doctor," said Emily.

Filip nodded as he stirred the teapot. A pungent smell filled the air, of tea leaves and tree bark and bitter herbs. "Roman has spent many years studying the illness. He has a theory that it can only be spread by actually living, day-by-day, with someone who is dying of ze plague. Roman says he sees ze most cross-infection among people who are caring for ze sick – ze mothers, ze husbands, ze nurses."

"So, you can't catch it just by sitting next to someone?" Ben asked.

Filip shook his head. "That would be very unlikely," he said.

Jack had been thinking of something else – Henry. "Can you catch it by being bitten?"

Again Filip shook his head. "No, if you are bitten by a lampir, you will almost certainly die. But from loss of blood, because a lampir will drink your blood until you are dead, not from infection. Ze only way to *become* a lampir yourself is to catch ze illness. It is *possible* to catch the plague from a lampir – I haf heard of it happening – but it is very rare and it is not passed in ze bite." He placed the teapot in the middle of the table and gave Jack a reassuring pat on the shoulder. "Do not worry about your friend Henry. A few days rest, a few cups of good Polish tea, and he will almost certainly recover. Now, who here would like tea?"

"Yes, please. . ." they all said absently.

Filip poured treacly black tea into all four glasses.

"I wonder where the plague came from all those centuries ago?" Emily wondered aloud.

"As to that," Filip responded, setting the teapot down again. "*That* is not a nice story. In ancient times there was a feudal lord who ruled over many towns and villages in Poland. His name was Count Casimir Lampirska."

"Lampirska. . ." Ben muttered.

Filip's mouth twisted. "Yes. Lampirska . . . lampir. You see ze connection."

Emily's face was white and strained. "The lampirs were named after him. But why?"

"Count Casimir sought eternal life, so he and his barons began to dabble in ze Black Arts. As ze stories of Lampirska's dark magic began to spread throughout ze land, followers flocked to ze count's banner – ze desperate, ze greedy, ze sinful, and ze downright evil. In his castle, high in ze mountains, these followers conducted many terrible rituals in their quest for eternal life, all under ze command of Count Casimir and his barons. And ze local people lived in fear, because ze count's followers stole so many children that ze villages in Casimir's territory became like ghost towns. . ."

Filip lowered his voice so that the friends had to lean forward to hear him better.

"Even today," he murmured softly, "Polish mothers will speak Count Casimir's name only in a whisper, for fear that his spirit may hear them and come to steal their babies."

Ben, Jack and Emily exchanged horrified glances across the table. "The count stole babies for his experiments?" Ben asked.

Filip nodded. "And these experiments eventually bore

fruit, but at a terrible price. Ze count achieved eternal life, but it was a strange half-life. He and his followers existed in ze shadow world, no longer living but not yet dead. And worst of all –" Cinska shuddered – "worst of all, they had to drink ze blood of ze living to survive. Thus was ze lampir created. And ze lampir plague soon followed."

CHAPTER FOURTEEN

A shocked, breathless silence filled the room as the friends mulled over Filip's words.

Filip placed a bowl of sugar lumps on the table and began to pass around the glasses of steaming black tea. "Tea," he said firmly. "You are in need of something to restore you, yes?"

He helped himself to one of the sugar lumps from the bowl and propped it between his front teeth. Still holding the sugar lump there, he sipped his tea, letting the black fluid wash over the sugar.

Emily took a sip of her own tea and immediately regretted it. It was horrible – so bitter that she had to stop herself from spitting it all over the tabletop. No wonder Cinska drank it with a sugar lump in his mouth! Seeing that the others were just about to try theirs, she grinned and watched to see how they would react.

She didn't have long to wait. Jack's face went bright red and he exploded in a fit of coughing. His hand shot out and plunged into the sugar bowl. He seized a handful of sugar lumps and practically *threw* them into his tea-glass.

Beside him, Ben's nose wrinkled and his eyes watered alarmingly as he gasped bravely, "Lovely tea, Filip!" Ben coughed and set his tea carefully back down on the table. "If the count and his barons achieved their goal – does that mean they're still roaming around Poland, drinking people's blood?" he enquired.

"No." Filip drained his tea-glass and poured himself some more. "They ruled for many years, it is true. Nobody could fight them, although many tried. But then a curious thing began to happen. A handful of people were infected by ze plague, just like everyone else. But instead of dying, these people recovered. They were able to fight off ze disease and become healthy once more. Some of their descendants also had this remarkable ability. Within a few generations these few families did not even fall ill. They had become immune to ze lampir plague!"

"Immune. . ." Jack muttered. "That means the illness stopped having an effect on them, don't it?"

"It does," Filip confirmed. "And it meant that these people were able to fight lampirs. They destroyed many of them. In time, they became part of folktale and legend. People called them 'dhampirs'."

"So did a dhampir make the Dhampir Bell?" Emily asked.

"Exactly so," Filip nodded. "Ze Dhampir Bell was created by a very powerful dhampir. It was forged several hundred years ago in ze fires of a foundry on ze banks of ze River Wisla. Ze bell is an old weapon in ze fight against lampirs. You see, when ze bell is rung and a person recites a particular incantation at ze same time, then ze bell will force ze infected dead back to their graves and imprison them there so that they cannot rise with ze next moon. Ze dhampir who created ze bell imprisoned hundreds . . . no, *thousands* of lampirs in this way! Sadly, ze incantation is now forgotten."

"A dhampir sounds like a useful friend to have," Ben mused. "Are there many of them?"

"Unfortunately they were very rare," Cinska told him. "Probably one or two families only. Nobody knows why they had this immunity when everyone else was dying around them. Perhaps their blood was stronger. Maybe there was something special in their bodies which gave them ze ability to fight ze plague." He shrugged. "I do not know. What I do know is that whatever was in their blood was poisonous to lampirs. A lampir can never drink ze blood of a dhampir. And ze lampir knows this – he will shy away from a dhampir, as if he senses that ze dhampir means danger."

"So, why don't you round up all the dhampirs and get them to fight the lampirs?" Jack asked.

"A good idea, you would think. But it is not as simple as that, my friend," Filip replied sadly. "Even in ze beginning there were not many dhampirs, and over ze centuries their numbers haf dwindled. Eventually they died out. Ze last man thought to haf dhampir blood in his veins died almost thirty years ago, in a monastery in Warsaw."

Ben fiddled thoughtfully with his tea-glass. "So with the last dhampir gone, there's nobody left to fight the lampirs?"

"Nobody," Filip agreed. "That is why ordinary people, like myself, must stir ze Polish into action – to make them take greater care and protect themselves. Unfortunately, not everyone accepts that ze threat is real."

Ben frowned. "They don't believe you?"

"Some do," Filip said. "Those who remember ze old ways and who believe ze legends. But others have become careless. They live in ze modern, rational world. Take my brother, Roman, for instance. He does not believe in ze lampir, just ze plague. A doctor with dozens of sick patients has no time for myths."

Filip gave a tight half-smile. "He has that in common with your Sir Peter Walker. Roman also says that I believe too much in folktales. But he cannot argue with ze facts. And ze facts are that people are dying of this plague, and have been for centuries."

"Surely the dhampirs kept it under control?" Jack asked.

"They did to a large extent," Filip agreed. "Cases were

rare, and outbreaks would usually happen only in small villages where people knew that ze bodies must be burned, not buried, to stop them rising as lampirs."

Emily swallowed hard. "Burned? That's terrible," she whispered.

"But it worked," Cinska said. "Ze plague was kept under control. However, since ze death of ze last dhampir, ze illness has begun to take hold in Poland again. That is why ze Dhampir Bell is so important. It will be a useful weapon if ze incantation can only be rediscovered!"

"Do you think it can be?" Ben enquired.

Filip nodded. "I believe so, with enough research. But in the meantime ze Dhampir Bell must be kept safe. And it should *never* haf been rung!"

"So that is what brought you to England!" Emily said, guessing what had happened. "You came to try and retrieve the Dhampir Bell?"

"Indeed. But I was too late," Filip sighed. "That strutting peacock of a man, he was determined to ring ze bell!"

"Why was that such a terrible thing to do?" Ben asked.

"Because when ze bell is rung, but the incantation is not chanted, a terrible thing happens," Filip explained gravely. "With that melodious chime, every lampir which has ever been imprisoned by ze bell will awake. They will break out of their graves when ze moonlight shines upon them, and come after their relatives. And not only that –" here Filip's voice dropped to a whisper – "not only that, but lampirs who are close enough to hear ze bell are drawn towards it. They cannot resist its wondrous chime."

There was a moment's silence, broken only by a piece of coal popping in the stove. Filip shifted restlessly on his stool. "So not only has ze lampir plague now spread to London, but lampirs in Poland haf been set free!"

"Then it's not just Henry's Uncle Jerzy," Jack said softly. "There will be more of them."

"Many more," agreed Filip. "You must be on your guard and listen for ze sound that indicates a lampir is nearby."

"What sound?" Ben asked.

"A lampir makes a 'death rattle'. Like this. . ." Filip picked up his glass and swigged back a mouthful of tea. Then he dropped his chin on to his chest and sucked air in through his nose. A moment later a terrible sound came from deep in his throat – a rasping, guttural growl.

"That's the noise the creature made in the cemetery last night!" Emily cried.

Ben nodded. "And Henry's Uncle Jerzy made it, too."

Filip fell silent, massaging his throat with one hand as if making the "death rattle" had hurt. "More tea, I think," he said. "Shall I make a fresh pot?"

"I'm fine," Jack replied hastily.

"Me too!" Ben exclaimed.

"None for me," Emily put in. "But it was very nice, thank you."

Jack leant forward thoughtfully. "I've been thinking about the disturbed graves in the cemetery – that wasn't grave-robbers, was it? It was lampirs. . ."

Ben bit his lip. "But if there are so many lampirs climbing out of graves, why don't we see them? Surely they'd be walking the streets looking for victims."

"They probably are," Cinska said firmly. "But during ze day, they are only shadows. And most are probably still in ze early stages, where they have to drink from their relatives. They will stay in ze area where their families live. They won't be hunting through ze rest of ze city yet."

"Well," Ben said, brightly, "at least people are safe in the daytime!"

This was greeted by such a doom-laden silence from Filip Cinska that all three friends looked at him expectantly.

He sighed. "I wish that was true." He peered through the grimy window at the street below. "Come here, my friends. I will show you something. . ."

The three friends crossed the room and pressed their noses to the window, peering down into Tiler's Alley. It was not far off midday, and bright winter sunshine shone down on to the cobblestones. A handful of children had come out to play. Their happy laughter echoed faintly up to the window.

"I can see some boys playing with marbles. . ." Emily said hesitantly. "And there's a woman on her knees, scrubbing the doorstep. But everything looks normal."

Jack and Ben agreed. "There's nothing out of the ordinary down there," Ben said slowly.

Filip looked at him. "All is normal, you think. But look closer. . ."

He leaned over their shoulders to point out a skinny little child skipping about at the far end of the alley. She was a tiny pixie of a girl, about six years old, with silky white-blonde hair that tumbled almost to her waist.

"What's so strange about her?" Emily asked. "She's just—"

But then Jack gripped her arm tightly. "Look at her shadow, Emily!" he urged.

So Emily looked, and her heart missed a beat. Because instead of the slight, nimble shadow that should have been cast by the little girl, spilling across the cobbles behind her loomed the black shadow of a large man with hunched shoulders and clawed hands.

CHAPTER FIFTEEN

"A lampir's hiding in her shadow!" Jack cried. "It's stalking her. And when it gets dark and the creature can take human form. . ."

". . .she'll be dead," Ben finished for him.

Emily drew back from the window. "That poor little girl – we've got to help her!"

Filip shook his head sadly, his eyes fixed on the ominous shadow down in Tiler's Alley. "There is no way to help her," he said.

"There must be," Jack insisted. "We . . . we could go down there and stay with her. Then when it gets dark and the lampir takes on human-form, we'll set fire to it . . . burn it!" His voice rose eagerly. "We could do that to every lampir we can find!"

"An admirable goal, my friend," Filip said. "But you cannot possibly destroy every lampir individually. There are just too many."

"But what if we could get all the lampirs together?"

Ben said, feeling a rush of hope as an idea began to form. "What if we could lure them all to one place? Say – a shed, or a warehouse, somewhere like that." He clenched his fist as the idea crystallized in his mind. "If we burnt down the building, they would all be destroyed at once!"

"But how would we do that?" Jack asked. "You don't just waltz up to a lampir and say, 'Excuse me, but d'you mind coming with me? I want to lock you up with your mates and burn you all to a crisp!'"

"No," Ben replied patiently. "But Filip said that lampirs can't resist the sound of the Dhampir Bell. We could use it as a lure."

"That could work," Filip said. "But it would be dangerous. If they get close enough then ze lampirs will try to snatch ze Dhampir Bell, because they know it has power over them." He rubbed his chin thoughtfully. "But it is a good plan. . ."

"We'd have to do it soon," Jack put in. "While there aren't many lampirs."

"It's a great idea, Ben," Emily said, smiling. But then her face clouded. "Wait a minute, though," she said slowly. "If you lure all the lampirs to one place and burn them, that will get rid of the dead who have already risen from their graves. But what about all the other infected people who haven't actually died and turned into lampirs yet?"

"Good point, Em," Ben admitted, frowning. "What would we do about them?"

Filip, however, clapped his hands in delight. "Finally, I haf some good news for you!" he declared, beaming. "If a lampir is destroyed, then happily ze illness infecting him dies too. So every other person who ever caught ze disease from him is instantly cured!"

Emily looked at the little Polish man in surprise. "So if Ben's plan was successful, and we killed all the lampirs in London, there would be mass recoveries from the plague?"

"Just so," Filip confirmed.

"Then what are we waiting for?" Emily darted to the table and snatched up her gloves. "We must go and get the Dhampir Bell."

"Where do you plan to get that, Em?" Ben asked, following her as she made her way to the door.

"The Royal Institution!" she exclaimed. "I heard Sir Peter say that the Eastern European artefacts would remain on display there until the New Year." She headed down the stairs in a flurry of petticoats. "Sir Peter's going to be there today, doing another talk. We can ask him to let us borrow the bell."

"But he's not simply going to let us take it, is he?" Ben pointed out, as he followed her downstairs, with Jack and Filip Cinska right behind him. "Not when he's spent all that money restoring it."

"He might," Emily insisted. "If we tell him it's for research purposes. We can say that we're working on something independently of Uncle Edwin. You know how Sir Peter likes to outdo his professional rivals – if we can persuade him that we'll share our findings with him instead of Edwin, then he's almost bound to let us borrow it!"

At the bottom of the stairs, Emily threw the front door open and the four of them emerged on to the street outside. "Come on," she urged. "There's no time to waste! The Royal Institution opens its doors at midday. If we hurry, we'll get there just in time to see Sir Peter before he starts his talk." She turned to Filip. "We'll let you know how we get on!" And then she was gone, heading off up Tiler's Alley with a determined expression on her face.

Filip watched her go, one eyebrow raised. "She is like a whirlwind, that girl," he said.

"You're not wrong there," Jack replied with a big grin, as he and Ben set off after her.

CHAPTER SIXTEEN

As they hurried along Tiler's Alley, Ben checked his pockets and came up with a handful of change. "Just enough to get us to the Royal Institution in a hansom," he said. "Come on."

But Jack wasn't listening. His attention had been caught by the little blonde girl they'd seen from Filip Cinska's window. She had stopped skipping and was hopping down a hopscotch grid that some of the other children had chalked on the cobbles. She was singing a nursery rhyme: *To see a fine lady upon a white horse. . ."*

Jack hurried across to a nearby tree and snapped off one of the brittle lower branches. Next he darted over to a brazier, elbowing his way through the group of old men warming themselves by the fire. He thrust the branch deep into the flames.

"Fire, remember?" he called to Ben.

As soon as the tips of the branch were aflame, Jack danced towards the little girl.

As he drew near, Jack whirled the branch so that it made great orange rings in the air. The little girl stopped to watch.

"With rings on her fingers and bells on her toes. . ." Jack sang. *"She shall have* FIRE *wherever she goes!"*

"Again!" the girl cried, clapping her hands and laughing.

"Your wish is my command," Jack replied, and he danced around her, twirling the crackling branch, one moment high above her head, the next down low by her feet. Instantly the big black shadow that loomed behind her seemed to shrivel and shrink.

Yeah, Jack thought. *Scared now, ain't you?*

"What's your name?" he asked the little girl.

"Beatrice," she replied, her eyes following Jack's every move.

"Beatrice, eh?" Jack spelled out her name in huge orange letters, while keeping a close watch on her shadow. Suddenly, he thrust the flaming branch downwards so that sparks scattered across the cobbles.

The lampir shadow flickered, then detached itself from Beatrice's feet and slid away across the cobbles to join the shadows of a nearby building. In its place was the girl's own shadow, small and dainty with rippling skirts.

Relief washed over Jack. He turned to Beatrice and smiled.

"Again!" she demanded, laughing up at him.

"One last dance," he agreed, "if you promise to run straight home to your ma afterwards!" He didn't want the lampir coming back after he'd gone.

"I promise."

So Jack whirled the branch round and round, faster and faster, creating huge fiery arcs in the air before returning to thrust it deep into the brazier.

"He's off his head!" chuckled one of the old men.

"Completely barmy," another agreed.

Jack grinned and pretended to take off an imaginary hat so that he could perform an elaborate, courtly bow for the little girl. "Your servant, Miss Beatrice," he said. "Now run away home to your ma."

Laughing, the girl danced away down the alley and Jack hurried over to where Emily and Ben were waiting. Ben smiled and patted his friend on the back.

"That was really kind of you," Emily said warmly. And she linked her arm through Jack's as they made their way out on to Tooley Street to flag down a cab.

When they arrived at the Royal Institution half an hour later, Jack was surprised to see a group of six or eight burly men standing on the steps talking together. They were wearing a uniform of heavy boots, dark stovepipe hats, and blue frock coats fastened with gleaming brass buttons and wide leather belts. Several black four-wheeled carriages were parked at the kerb.

"Do they always have coppers at the Institution,

then?" Jack whispered to Ben uneasily. Although his pickpocketing years were now behind him, he could never quite shake off the guilty feeling that policemen gave him.

Ben shook his head. "Never seen them here before," he muttered. "Let's go and find out what's going on."

They ran up the stairs and through the doors. Once inside, Jack glanced around with interest. So this was the Royal Institution, he thought. Very grand! Acres of black and white floor tiles, graceful potted palm trees, and sweeping marble staircases. If it hadn't been for the pictures of steam engines and ships on the walls, Jack reflected, he'd have thought he was in an expensive hotel rather than a place devoted to science and invention.

He felt Ben nudge him. "There's Sir Peter, over there."

Sir Peter was standing on the bottom step of one of the marble staircases. He was wearing an expensive-looking black coat and a high collared shirt, which looked too tight for his fleshy neck. His monocle glittered in his left eye socket as he directed a dozen clerks, sending them scuttling in all directions. "Pack up all the artefacts!" he cried. "Everything! I don't want a single item left here. It's quite obviously unsafe."

Sir Peter turned to an elderly, white-haired gentleman standing beside him. "Really," he said. "As Director of the Institution, you must review your security arrangements with all haste. It's simply not good enough, you know!"

"But the Royal Institution is one of the safest buildings in London," protested the director.

"Tell that to a man who hasn't just had his priceless historical artefacts vandalized!" retorted Sir Peter.

He spotted Ben, Jack and Emily and raised one arm in greeting. "Ah, Benedict, my dear boy! No doubt you've heard of this calamity on the grapevine and are coming to offer me your condolences!"

Sir Peter broke free of the gaggle of assistants who surrounded him and strode to meet them. He laid a heavy arm across Ben's shoulders. "Terrible business. Simply dreadful. Come with me and see the damage!"

Leaving Jack and Emily to scurry in his wake, Sir Peter marched off with Ben. They made their way upstairs and along a corridor. Eventually they came to a set of double doors where another policeman stood guard.

"What's going on, sir?" Ben asked Sir Peter.

"A break-in, that's what," the historian replied. "Bunch of ruffians broke in here during the night. Eastern Europeans, I'll be bound, eager to take back a few of the antiquities I purchased in Poland. Dashed sensitive lot, these foreigners. I've seen it before! They get quite uppity, you know. Don't seem to understand that if I pay good money for a thing, then it's mine. A simple commercial transaction!"

"I see," Ben said faintly.

"The brutes obviously knew exactly what they were

119

looking for – they came straight up here to the room where all my Eastern European items are on display. Didn't touch anything else on the way. Not a thing!" Sir Peter took out his monocle and swung it mournfully on its chain as they reached the double doors. "Oh, they knew what they were looking for all right. And when they couldn't get it, they smashed everything in sight. Look at this!"

He threw the door open to reveal a scene of complete devastation: chairs splintered, glass shattered, display cases tipped over, their contents spilled across the floor. A couple of policemen poked about amid the mess. One of Sir Peter's assistants was busy wrapping up the few undamaged items and packing them into a wooden crate.

"This ain't good," Jack murmured. "What do you think the thieves were after?"

Sir Peter held up his monocle and peered at Jack through it, looking him up and down as if trying to work out who he was.

"This is my friend, Jack Harkett," Ben said hastily. "And you remember my sister, Emily."

"Ah yes." Sir Peter nodded, his glance barely reaching Emily's face before he clapped Jack on the shoulder. "Welcome, Jack. Any friend of Benedict's is a friend of mine. And you may well ask what the thieves were after, young man! You may well ask. Come with me and I'll show you."

Sir Peter led the way across the room, picking a careful path through the broken earthenware pots and scattered coins. He came to a halt in front of a huge wrought-iron box, about two feet wide and three feet high. A plaque on the front declared in big brass letters that it was a *Wellesley Forman Safe – Patented Against Fire and Theft*. Down one side was a row of the most enormous hinges that Jack had ever seen. Down the other side was a series of deep gouges and dents.

A policeman with bristling side-whiskers came crunching across the broken glass towards them. "Inspector Fisher asked me to let you know that we're no further forwards with our investigation I'm afraid, Sir Peter," he said apologetically. "But one of our experts has now had a chance to look at the safe. He's never seen the like of this damage before – says he reckons someone took a pickaxe to it. Someone very strong!"

"Strong, eh?" Sir Peter barked. "Then I trust you'll be sending constables to every building site between here and Whitechapel." He thought for a moment, then added, "Try the fairgrounds too. You get those so-called strongmen there, don't you? Round 'em all up and bring 'em in for questioning!"

The policeman looked dazed, and Jack felt quite sorry for him.

"I . . . I'm sure Inspector Fisher will be following every line of enquiry, sir," the policeman said, nervously fingering the silver whistle that dangled from his belt.

"But at the moment we're concentrating on motive, sir. Nothing has been taken, so the thieves must have been after whatever's in this safe."

"What *is* in the safe?" Ben asked hesitantly.

Sir Peter screwed his monocle into his left eye socket and puffed out his chest. "In this safe is my finest trophy," he replied. "The highlight of my lecture last night. My most prized—"

"The Dhampir Bell!" Emily exclaimed brightly, and then subsided as Sir Peter shot her a look of extreme distaste. "Sorry. . ."

"Silence is a virtue that all females would do well to espouse," Sir Peter muttered.

Jack grinned at the mutinous expression on Emily's face.

"But yes, as it happens, you are quite correct. The thieves were after the Dhampir Bell," Sir Peter confirmed.

Jack felt a jolt of alarm. The Dhampir Bell was the very thing they'd come to borrow – and thieves had almost snatched it from their grasp. Something flickered at the corner of his vision and he turned to look, but there was nothing there.

Sir Peter had drawn a key out of his coat pocket. He bent to unlock the safe. "All I can say is, thank heavens I had the foresight to lock the Dhampir Bell away last night, otherwise who knows where it would be by now. And it's irreplaceable, you know – utterly unique!"

Jack caught Ben's glance and knew immediately what his friend was thinking – if only Sir Peter knew *how* unique.

Sir Peter unlocked the safe. The damaged hinges creaked as he opened the door and Jack got his first glimpse of the Dhampir Bell. It was about the size of a small beer keg but made entirely of bronze, and it was somehow less grand than he'd expected. Jack felt slightly disappointed.

But then Sir Peter lifted the bell out of the safe, and a shaft of sunlight caught the polished surface and made it gleam. Some kind of inscription cut into the rim seemed to sparkle and flash as Sir Peter tilted the bell this way and that, inspecting it for possible damage.

Jack found himself holding his breath. The Dhampir Bell was beautiful. There was something about it that he couldn't quite put his finger on, something almost magical. . .

He felt the atmosphere in the room around him change. The light seemed to shift and the shadows rippled. Jack felt the hairs on the back of his neck rise. *What is going on?* he wondered. He glanced around to see whether anyone else had noticed anything strange, but everybody was concentrating on the bell.

Eventually the feeling subsided and Jack shrugged. *Must be all these coppers making me nervous*, he thought, eyeing the policeman who was still standing beside Sir Peter.

Sir Peter placed the Dhampir Bell reverently on the top of the safe and dusted it off with his silk handkerchief. "Undamaged," he said, obviously relieved. He beckoned one of his assistants over. "Kingsley, wrap the bell and have it put in my carriage. I shall take it to Windsor with me tonight."

Tonight? Jack glanced at Emily. "So, what are the chances of him letting us borrow the bell?" he whispered.

Emily pursed her lips. "Non-existent," she said glumly. "I'm going to talk to that policeman and find out more about who they think broke in here. Coming with me?"

Jack shook his head vehemently. "Nah," he said. "Me and policemen ain't a good mix."

As Emily moved away, Jack wandered over to the window and peered down at the street below. The police were milling about along with some of Sir Peter's clerks, who bustled up and down the steps, carrying boxes to one of the carriages waiting at the kerb.

Jack turned around and leant against the windowsill. What a mess the room was. He was glad he didn't have to help clear it up. Mind you, there were plenty of people working on it. Jack idly began to count them. Six, eight, ten, and someone who was half hidden behind a tall display case. Jack wouldn't have noticed him except that his shadow stretched all the way out across the floor.

Jack stepped forwards, curious to see the man who was casting such a shadow. He was surprised to find that the fellow was quite small. Jack checked the position of the sun and looked again at the young man's shadow. It really was enormous, with a hunched back and claw-fingers – *just like little Beatrice's*.

Jack's heart began to pound. He looked around, paying closer attention to the shadows now, and realized with a thrill of dread that there were at least a dozen lampirs in the room.

CHAPTER SEVENTEEN

Ben crossed the room to Emily. "I don't know if you heard that," he said, "but Sir Peter's hauling the whole collection off to Windsor – that's more than twenty miles away!"

Emily had been gazing at Jack – and Jack, Ben noticed, was preoccupied with a policeman who was standing by a tall bookcase.

"What's the matter with Jack?" Emily asked, frowning. "He looks worried about something."

"I shouldn't worry about that," Ben said with a smile. "Jack has an irrational fear of men in blue coats! But listen, Em, we have a bigger problem than that. How are we going to get the Dhampir Bell if it's in Windsor?"

"Don't worry," Emily replied. "We've been in worse predicaments than this before. Just follow my lead. . ." She took Ben's arm and marched him towards Sir Peter with a purposeful stride.

The historian was standing with an important-looking

policeman, who was obviously in charge of the investigation. The two of them seemed to be having a competition to see who could puff their chest out the most. One of Sir Peter's assistants hovered in the background, wringing his hands and looking anxious.

"But the Dhampir Bell is evidence," the policeman was saying. "We are investigating a crime here. And you cannot remove evidence from the scene of a crime!"

"I, sir, shall do as I wish!" Sir Peter responded. "These artefacts are not evidence – they are priceless pieces of history. And they belong to me. If I say they're going to Windsor, then they're going to Windsor."

"Oh, I absolutely agree with you, Sir Peter," Emily interrupted loudly. "It's the only safe place for them, after all. I know my father always used to say the security at Brayleigh Court was second to none."

Sir Peter looked surprised, but pleased. "Why, thank you . . . er, Emma. Thank you for your support."

"It's Emily," said Emily. And Ben could see that she was gritting her teeth and forcing a smile.

At her interruption, the policeman had turned a mottled shade of red. "Well, really, Miss—"

But Sir Peter cut him off. "You're wasting your breath, Inspector Fisher. My mind is quite made up. Windsor it is."

The Inspector favoured Sir Peter with one last glare, turned on his heel and stalked away.

"Right, then." Sir Peter snapped his fingers at the

assistant who was still hovering nearby. "That's settled. Now let's finish up here as quickly as possible."

"Yes, Sir Peter," the assistant said. "I will take the Dhampir Bell myself." He scurried away.

"Oh, Sir Peter," Emily gushed, "you do have such an air of authority. Ben and I always feel we're learning so much when we're with you – not just about history, but about *life*."

Ben goggled at his sister. What on earth was she *saying*?

"You know, Sir Peter. . ." Emily went on. "I was only thinking the other day that it was rather reckless of Uncle Edwin to have gone off on a jaunt to Warsaw without taking more elaborate precautions for the safety of his *own* collection. I mean, he hasn't got much – just a few books and the odd prehistoric finger-bone, nothing to compare with your own amazing collection of artefacts – but even so." She tutted and shook her head.

Ben wondered if his sister had gone slightly mad.

"I totally agree with you!" Sir Peter boomed pompously. "But I have always suspected Edwin to be rather a careless fellow."

"Sometimes I wonder what Father would make of it all," Emily sighed. She pressed the tip of one finger to the corner of her eye. "I do miss him so. And being here in London is a dreadful strain, isn't it, Ben?" She gave Ben a sharp jab with her elbow. "We find reminders of him everywhere. . ."

"Oh, yes," said Ben hastily. "Yes, we do."

"My poor girl," Sir Peter said, looking confused and rather uncomfortable. "You . . . er. . . Oh, I say. Oh, dear me. Please, don't cry." Clumsily he reached out and patted Emily on the head.

"I'm sorry," she gulped. "I just wish there was somewhere we could go to get away from it all. You know – a little holiday away from the hustle and bustle of the city."

Ben suddenly cottoned on to Emily's plan. He grinned, then quickly organized his features into an expression of pathetic longing. "Oh, yes," he said. "Wouldn't that be wonderful, Em? A few days in the countryside."

Beside him, Emily's face brightened, as if she'd just remembered something. "Oh, Sir Peter, only yesterday you mentioned that we might come to stay with you at Brayleigh Court. I think Ben and I would be delighted to accept your invitation. It's just the other side of Windsor, isn't it?"

Sir Peter looked a bit taken aback. "Er, yes. Yes it is."

Emily clapped her hands, her tears suddenly forgotten. "Oh, that's a wonderful idea. Sir Peter, you are *so* kind. And so clever and knowledgeable – isn't he, Ben? Father always said we could learn so much from you, if only we had time to listen."

"Well, we've got time now," Ben put in. "We could come tomorrow, couldn't we, Em? What do you say, Sir Peter?"

"Well, er. . ." Sir Peter looked as if he'd been run over

by a galloping coach-and-four. "Well, no time like the present, I suppose."

"Then that's settled," Emily said firmly. "We'll go home immediately and make arrangements with our housekeeper." She beamed up at Sir Peter. "We'll catch the first train from Paddington Station and be with you tomorrow – say, mid-morning? Excellent. Goodbye!" And leaving Sir Peter looking somewhat stunned, Emily and Ben hurried away to rejoin Jack.

"So far so good, Em," Ben murmured. "The Dhampir Bell will be at Sir Peter's house in Windsor, and so will we. But how are we going to persuade him to let us borrow it?"

"We'll figure that out on the way home," Emily said happily. "Three heads are better than one, aren't they, Jack?"

But Jack didn't reply. He simply grasped Emily's wrist and Ben's sleeve and dragged them towards the door. "We've got to get out of here fast," he urged. "While we've still got our own shadows!"

Outside in the fresh air, Jack walked a complete circle around Emily and Ben, glaring at the cobbles beneath their feet.

"Jack, what's wrong?" Ben asked.

"You're acting very strangely." Emily reached out and pressed the palm of her hand to Jack's forehead. "Have you got a fever?"

Jack shook his head. "No fever," he said. "And I ain't crazy, neither. It's just that there were lampirs in that room and I wanted to make sure none of 'em had hidden in your shadows."

Emily and Ben gaped at him. "Lampirs?" Ben glanced back over his shoulder at the Royal Institution's imposing front doors. "In *there*?"

"In there," Jack confirmed grimly. "Reckon they were spying on the Dhampir Bell. I was thinking about it while you were talking to Sir Peter. Filip Cinska told us that lampirs are drawn to the bell's chime. Obviously, at first, the lampirs would've gone looking for their relatives, like Jerzy did, so's they could feed. But then they would have been drawn to the bell, when Sir Peter rang it. And now they know it's got power over them, stands to reason they're going to want that bell. . ."

"So you think they came here and broke in?" Emily asked.

"Of course, lampirs tried to steal the bell!" Ben exclaimed. "That's why it looked as if someone had attacked it with a pickaxe."

Jack nodded. "Except it wasn't a pickaxe. It was lampirs with the strength of ten men."

"Thank goodness for Wellesley Forman Safes!" Emily declared. "Or they'd have beaten us to it."

"They must have been trying to open it for hours," Ben said. "And then the sun came up. There's no protection in that room, what with all those huge windows."

"So they were turned into shadows," Emily finished eagerly. Then she shuddered and glanced behind at her own slender shadow. "How horrible. But Jack, how did you realize?"

"I spotted a shadow that was out of place," Jack explained. "Now, tell me. What's going on with Sir Peter? You two were looking pretty pleased with yourselves up there."

During the journey home, Emily and Ben filled Jack in on their conversation with the historian.

"So you're going to stay with Sir Peter for a day or two," Jack said with a grin. "That's good. But how are you going to persuade him to part with the bell? He don't look like the sort of gent who'd be convinced by stories of lampirs."

"He'd laugh us out of the house!" Emily agreed. "Much better to talk about thieves, I think. Perhaps we could try to convince him that they might target his country house and make an even bigger mess than they did at the Institution. Maybe we could remind him about the madman who interrupted his lecture – not mentioning that it was Filip Cinska, of course."

"Good idea," Jack said with a nod. "Let him think there's a whole gang of lunatic Poles who're desperate to get their bell back!"

"And if that doesn't work," Ben put in. "We'll just have to steal the Dhampir Bell ourselves!"

"What?" Jack goggled at him. "*You*, turn *thief*?"

"Why not?" Ben suddenly looked very serious. "Sometimes you have to do the right thing, even if it's wrong." He frowned, as if he'd confused even himself. "If you know what I mean."

Jack grinned. "I know what you mean," he said. "But thieving a great big bell like that from some cove's country estate won't be an easy matter. You're going to need some help."

Ben nodded. "Well, that's where you come in. I was thinking that you might come to Windsor and stay in a coaching inn or something. Em and I could sneak out and let you know how things are going, and if necessary you can help us stage a break-in."

"You make it all sound so simple," Jack laughed.

"It is simple," Ben replied. "It has to be. Just keep your mind on the fact that by this time tomorrow, one way or another, we need to have the Dhampir Bell."

By teatime, Ben and Emily had finalized their arrangements for the journey to Berkshire. Mrs Mills had accepted their explanation about going to stay with Sir Peter without question. Her only comment had been, "Windsor? Well, I suppose it makes a change from gallivanting off to Paris!"

She then whipped the household up into a frenzy, telling Evans to stoke up the range and set the flat irons to heat. Tillet was sent up to the attic to bring down trunks, carpet bags and an enormous hat-box, despite

Ben's protests that they were only going for a couple of days and wouldn't really need to take more than two changes of clothes.

"Nonsense, Master Ben!" Mrs Mills declared. "An invitation to stay in a gentleman's country residence? Why, there will be parlour games and music recitals and walks in the woodland. . . You'll need an outfit for every occasion. And no well-to-do young person can be seen downstairs after the dinner gong has sounded in anything but full evening dress! That will be tailcoat, trousers, cravat, collar studs, gloves for you two boys. . ." Mrs Mills had assumed that Jack was going with them, and nobody had bothered to correct her. Off she went, bustling along the landing to throw open the door to Emily's bedroom. "And nothing but taffeta and lace for Miss Emily!"

Bemused but smiling, the three friends watched as Mrs Mills began to whirl petticoats about until Emily's bed looked as if it had survived a snowstorm.

By morning everything had been pressed and packed with military efficiency.

"We should have sent word to Filip, to tell him what's going on," Emily said thoughtfully over breakfast.

"I'll do that," Jack offered. "I'll go now, and meet you at the railway station."

An hour later, Ben and Emily were on their way, squeezed into the corner of a Great Western Railway carriage bound for Windsor Central Station. Three carpet bags and a big blue hat-box were stowed in the overhead luggage rack.

"I hope Jack isn't going to miss the train," Emily said anxiously, as the guard blew his whistle.

But just then Jack appeared at the door of their compartment. And he wasn't alone. Behind him stood Filip Cinska.

CHAPTER EIGHTEEN

Ben felt a grin stretch his face from ear to ear. "Filip!" he cried, as the train began to move. "What are you doing here?"

"I am come to help you, my friends," Filip replied. He was dressed as usual in his ancient tailcoat and striped trousers, topped off by a grey overcoat that looked two sizes too big for him. Today, however, he'd shaved his chin and made an effort to brush his wild blond hair, parting it on one side and smoothing it down with macassar oil. "Many hands make light work," he said with a smile, coming into the compartment and sliding the door closed. "So here I am!"

A great cloud of steam swept past the window, and Emily grinned. "Oh, if we weren't on such a serious mission, this might almost be fun!"

They drew into Windsor Station an hour later, with a view of the imposing royal castle set against a winter-grey sky.

Jack pressed his nose to the window. "Blimey," he murmured. "Look at that!"

After arranging to meet Ben and Emily at the gatehouse to Brayleigh Court at dusk that evening, Filip and Jack headed straight for the nearest inn. Ben and Emily took a coach to Sir Peter's country estate.

"Brayleigh Court, is it?" the driver said, knowledgeably. "Sir Peter Walker's place. He's one of Windsor's most famous residents – after Her Majesty the Queen, o' course! Been here before have you?"

"We have," Ben said. "But not for years."

The man soon filled them in on the details, telling them all about Brayleigh Court and its twelve acres of lawns and woodland as he loaded their bags. "Beautiful, it is," he said. "And I've heard it's stuffed full of antiques and the like. But you'll see that for yourselves when you get there. It ain't far."

And it wasn't. Two miles out of Windsor the coach took a sharp right turn, swept through an imposing set of elaborate wrought-iron gates, and made its way up the long, tree-lined drive. Ben gazed out of the window. He saw a grand mansion with turrets and chimneys. A circular sweep of gravel in front crunched under the wheels of the coach.

The front doors were wide open and Sir Peter was waiting for them, flanked by two footmen who trotted down the steps and immediately began to unload the luggage from the back of the coach.

"Welcome!" boomed Sir Peter. He was wearing a tweed jacket and knickerbockers, with a high-collared cream shirt. A pair of tiny, silky-coated dogs milled about at his feet. They spotted the newcomers and came fussing down the steps, yapping and trying to nip everything in sight.

"Down, Priss! Down, Minty!" Sir Peter cried, but they ignored him completely and darted in and out of the coach wheels, getting under everybody's feet.

Sir Peter flapped his hands ineffectually at the little dogs, and then clapped Ben on the shoulder. "Lovely to see you, Benedict, my boy! Trust you had a good journey. Oh, and you of course, Emma, m'dear."

"*Emily*," said Emily through gritted teeth.

Priss and Minty seemed to have decided to concentrate all their efforts on ripping the hem of her petticoat to shreds, but Sir Peter took no notice of the tiny dogs.

"Reeves! Fellowes!" he cried, snapping his fingers at the scurrying footmen. "Unload the bags, will you?" He seemed oblivious to the fact that Reeves and Fellowes had already taken the luggage indoors and were now efficiently closing the coach door and tipping the driver.

Sir Peter drew Ben up the wide steps which led to the front door. "What d'you think of Brayleigh Court so far, my boy?"

"Very nice, sir," Ben replied, which was an

understatement. Brayleigh Court was impressive, and every bit as grand as Sir Peter had hinted.

"Built about fifty years ago. . ." Sir Peter drawled. "Neo-classical façade. More than forty rooms in all. Twelve bedrooms, three salons, and an Italianate ballroom on the first floor. Let's do a tour, shall we? I can show you the Long Gallery where I keep my collection. Bit of a mess in there at the moment, what with the sudden influx of artefacts yesterday. Perhaps you'd like to give me a hand later, eh? Label up a few swords or something!"

"Oh yes!" Ben said, looking forward to seeing the swords, but hoping Sir Peter wouldn't brag too much about how he'd acquired them. "Did everything make it here all right?" Ben asked, thinking particularly of the Dhampir Bell.

"All safe and sound. Come along, I'll show you around. Reeves, take darling Priss and Minty into the kitchens and give them a titbit, would you? Must be time for their cake and milk!"

"Yes, sir," said Reeves, bending down to wrestle the tiny terrors away from Emily's ankles.

Sir Peter's tour seemed to last for ever. He led Ben and Emily through room after room of antiques, paintings and tapestries. But eventually Ben and Emily found themselves in the Long Gallery, a wood-panelled corridor that cut through the heart of the house. The Gallery was protected by solid locked doors at each end and lit entirely by a series of gas lamps dotted along the walls. There were no windows because, Sir Peter told them, natural light caused such terrible damage to antiquities.

"Better to keep everything out of the sun if you can," he explained.

Good for preservation, thought Ben, but not ideal for burglaries. He and Emily would simply have to make sure that they persuaded Sir Peter to part with the Dhampir Bell. Because even with Jack and Cinska to help, Ben couldn't imagine how they were going to successfully fake a break-in to a locked room with no windows.

Polished display cases lined the long walls of the gallery, giving it the formal feel of a museum. Down the centre stood a row of glass-topped tables. Peering into the nearest, Ben saw a selection of curved sabres with tasselled handles. The next housed scraps of embroidery, clay pipes, and row upon row of tiny porcelain birds, their wingtips picked out in blue and gold.

The very last table was covered with books and polishing cloths and pieces of broken pottery.

"Repairs," Sir Peter told them apologetically. "My assistant, Kingsley, and I are doing what we can to restore the artefacts that the thieves damaged. Kingsley is down in the kitchens now, boiling up a solution of glaze and glue. Sadly these items will have no value on the open market, but they can still be useful as points of interest during a lecture."

"I see," Ben said.

As Sir Peter bent over the table to flick a speck of dust from the fragile neck of what had once been some kind of amphora, or wine carrier, Ben felt Emily's hand on his arm. He glanced up and saw her look meaningfully at a tall, slender cabinet with a glass front.

Inside, glowing softly in the gaslight, was the Dhampir Bell.

CHAPTER NINETEEN

Sir Peter saw Emily and Ben looking at the cabinet and smiled indulgently. "Ah, yes," he said. "The Dhampir Bell. Got it here safely after that terrible business."

"I'm pleased to see you've got it in a locked cabinet," Emily said approvingly. "It would be terrible if the thieves tried to break in here."

Sir Peter looked alarmed. "Do you think they might?" he asked nervously. Then he shook his head. "No! Quite impossible."

"Your security *is* very good," Emily agreed, checking the lock on the front of the cabinet. "But think of the devastation at the Institution. The police seemed to think that the thieves had pickaxes – imagine the damage they could do here!" She straightened up and surveyed the quiet tranquillity of the Long Gallery.

Sir Peter went pale, and Emily knew she had him worried. She pressed home her advantage. "Perhaps it might be better to speak to a representative of the Polish

142

community, perhaps offer the Dhampir Bell back to them?"

"Give it back?" Sir Peter exploded. His monocle flew out of his eye socket and he glared at Emily as if she were personally responsible for all his troubles. "Give it *back*? My finest trophy? I've never heard such nonsense in all my life! The Dhampir Bell belongs to me and it will stay at Brayleigh Court."

"But the thieves—" Ben put in.

"A pox on the thieves!" Sir Peter interrupted. "I'll defend myself and my property with my bare hands if need be." Sir Peter puffed himself up and clenched his fists in front of his face like a boxer. "I'll do battle with a hundred – no, a *thousand* – housebreakers! I could handle myself in a situation, you know! Once had a sparring match with one of the boxing team when I was at Eton."

Emily didn't dare look at Ben, who had quickly changed a snort of laughter into a cough. "Well," she said weakly. "Perhaps we won't worry too much about thieves, then."

"That's the spirit!" Sir Peter nodded vigorously.

He went to clap her on the back, pulled himself up short and patted her on the head instead. "Right. Who's ready for a spot of elevenses, then?"

The rest of the day was taken up with eating. Sir Peter seemed to think that food was the best medicine for all ailments. First they had elevenses, which consisted of vast plates of chocolate eclairs and Bath buns eaten in the morning room. Then, Sir Peter barely gave them time to walk out on to the stone terrace and catch their breath before he rounded them up for luncheon. To Emily and Ben's dismay, this was a huge meal of roast mutton and boiled beef, followed by a towering confection of cherries and whipped cream. Then they were whisked away to the billiard room to "pot a few shots" as Sir Peter put it.

Emily was allowed into the billiard room, but she wasn't included in the billiards – "Man's game, dear girl. Not for the gentler female of the species!" – so she contented herself with sitting in a huge, red leather armchair by the fire, leafing through magazines full of advertisements for macassar oil and nose-hair clippers. She kept half an eye on Sir Peter and Ben, and half an eye on the window. She was conscious of the fact that at sundown she and Ben would have to make their excuses and slip away to meet Jack and Filip Cinska.

When the carriage clock on the mantel chimed four, Emily shot Ben a meaningful look.

Ben straightened up and propped his billiard cue against the table. "Sir Peter, I wonder if it would be all right for Emily and me to take a walk outside. We're very keen to have a look at your lovely gardens."

"Emily. . . ?" For a moment Sir Peter looked as though he had no idea who Ben was talking about. But then his monocled eye swivelled across to the red leather armchair and he harrumphed and coughed and said, "Of course, dear boy. I believe a bracing constitutional is quite the thing these days. I'd come with you myself, but I really should go and see how Kingsley is getting on with repairing those artefacts. Will you be all right on your own?"

"Don't worry about us," Ben assured him hastily. "We're used to being alone. Come on, Em."

They wrapped up in warm coats, hats and scarves, and hurried outside. A tree-lined walk led them past Japanese-style water-gardens, with smooth boulders and creeping plants. Further on Emily gave a gasp of delight at the sight of a waterfall gushing over a series of steps cut into the rock. Then Ben found an interesting cluster of statues.

Eventually they spotted the imposing entrance to Brayleigh Court in the distance and ran towards it, arriving breathless to find Jack and Filip Cinska standing just outside the wrought-iron gates.

When they'd all caught up on the latest news – Jack telling Emily and Ben about their inn, and Emily explaining the whereabouts of the Dhampir Bell – a determined expression settled on Jack's face.

"So, what are we going to do?" he asked. "If Sir Peter ain't afraid of thieves, then we gotta work out how to take the bell ourselves. Or you could try telling him the truth, I suppose. If *he* knew what *we* know about lampirs, he'd be practically *begging* you to take the bell off his hands!"

Ben shook his head. "It's going to be a nigh on impossible task to persuade Sir Peter to believe in lampirs."

"What's our next move then?" Jack said with a frown. "We need the bell. Without it, we can't carry out the plan. . ."

"And the consequences of that don't bear thinking about!" Emily finished glumly.

"Maybe I could try?" Filip suggested hesitantly. "I could come with you, talk to Sir Peter, explain to him?"

Emily smiled. "It's a nice thought, Filip. But if Sir Peter gets so much as a glimpse of your face he'll start bellowing about foreigners and lunatics. He already thinks you're a madman – if you tell him everything you've told us he'll send out for the doctor and have you certified!"

"That's if he doesn't send for the police first," Ben added. "Last time he saw you, he was talking about Bedlam Hospital for the Criminally Insane!"

"Bedlam?" Jack shivered. "You don't want to be going there, Filip. I've heard they shaves off yer hair and chains you to the floor with nobody for company except rats."

Cinska sighed and all four of them stood in silence for a moment, trying to think of an alternative.

Eventually Emily sighed. "I think we're going to have

to try Jack's idea of telling the truth," she said. "Just as a last effort, before we resort to stealing the bell." She looked at Ben thoughtfully. "Perhaps *you* could talk to Sir Peter about the lampirs, Ben? He thinks the world of you. He's more likely to believe what you say."

Ben scraped the gravel with the toe of his boot, obviously thinking hard. At length he nodded. "All right then. I'll do it after tea this evening," he said. "I've got a few ideas of how to make it work. . ." he frowned and looked into the distance, where the house slumbered peacefully – white against the sunset, "but if Sir Peter doesn't believe me, then we'll have to come up with a way to steal the Dhampir Bell ourselves."

After an enormous tea, eaten in the Great Hall where a table roughly the size of Ben's whole bedroom in Bedford Square had been piled high with cucumber sandwiches and plates of sliced tongue, Sir Peter sat back and rubbed his stomach appreciatively. "Can't beat a good high tea!" he boomed. "Hope that'll see you through until dinner. I usually sup at eight o'clock – that all right for you? Good, good," he heaved his chair back from the head of the table. "Now then, let's find darling Priss and dear Minty."

The tiny dogs were under the enormous table, tearing an expensive damask napkin to shreds. Sir Peter scooped them up, one under each arm. "Come into the sitting room, Benedict, my boy," he said. "Let's roast our knees by the fire and I'll tell you a bit more about my time in India with the Maharajah of Mandrapur."

"Sounds wonderful!" Ben replied politely.

However, once in the sitting room, Ben settled himself into a comfortable chair opposite Sir Peter and gently steered the conversation from maharajahs to myths.

The sitting room was large and ornate, with gold velvet wallpaper, plush purple drapes at the windows, and a vast black marble fireplace. Tall candles set in ebony candelabra flickered on every surface, lighting up the antique furniture that dotted the room: leggy little tables, over-stuffed footstools, and a globe on a mahogany stand.

A set of French windows led out on to a wide terrace, and through the glass panes Ben could just make out the ghostly white shape of the stone balustrade, beyond which the twilit gardens stretched away into darkness.

The whole room had a gothic feel to it, Ben thought. He couldn't have set a better scene for his tale of lampirs. Even the enormous stag antlers, fixed high on the wall, cast eerie shadows that looked like lampir fingers creeping across the floor towards Sir Peter's feet.

"The thing with myths, dear boy," Sir Peter was saying, as he settled Priss and Minty on his lap, "is that the darn things get in the way of the truth."

"But what if some myths have grown out of the truth?" Emily enquired, from her place on a large gold sofa.

Sir Peter shrugged. "*Some* myths may have the seeds of truth in them. But the trick is knowing how to tell the difference between those that have their roots in truth and those that don't. Many myths are utter bunkum, and as scientists we have to be very wary of bunkum because it gets in the way of evidence!"

"My father would have agreed with that," Ben replied with a nod. "He was very disciplined about evidence-gathering."

"Harrison Cole was an admirable scientist!" Sir Peter agreed.

"But, it's interesting," Ben said, "when Father was travelling in Eastern Europe a few years ago, he was surprised to find that several of the stories he'd dismissed as folktales actually contained elements of truth. I think he was rather taken aback to discover that he couldn't entirely discredit some of the eyewitness accounts."

"Is that so?" Sir Peter raised an eyebrow.

Ben leant forward towards the fire so that his elbows were resting on his knees. "Father thought there might be a lot more truth to the old Polish folktales than any-one had previously suspected."

"Well, anything's possible, my boy," Sir Peter said sagely. "If Harrison found some truth to the tales, then I'd certainly like to hear it."

Ben held out his hands and let the firelight play over his fingertips. "Father heard a lot of stories about a plague which swept through Poland about four hundred years ago." He glanced at Sir Peter. "I believe you mentioned the subject during your lecture at the Royal Institution."

Sir Peter nodded. "Indeed I did. Glad to hear you were paying attention."

"Well," Ben continued, "Father decided to see if there was any documentation to support the stories. He found that various Polish history books mentioned a *real* plague, and they linked the spread of disease to the activities of a feudal lord, Count Casimir Lampirska—"

"Heard of him!" Sir Peter trumpeted. "Black-hearted fellow! The swine kidnapped children and locked them up in his castle. Hoodwinked a bunch of villainous barons into doing his dirty work, by all accounts – torture, murder, poison – a pretty mix of vile and unholy practices. . ."

"About as unholy as you can get according to the history books," Ben agreed. A candle guttered, then flared and Ben carefully lowered his voice slightly, so that Sir Peter had to lean forward to hear him. "It was Count Casimir's unholiness which led to the plague," Ben went on. "The pestilence fell upon the people of Poland, spreading from farmstead to farmstead and from village to village. Victims began to die of terrible symptoms – their fingernails went purple and their blood seemed to freeze in their veins. Whole families fled, but no one was safe. People died in their hundreds, but even after death the suffering did not end. When the moon next rose in the night sky, the dead turned into creatures called 'lampirs', and clawed their way out of the grave to stalk the streets seeking human blood."

Sir Peter gave a scornful snort. "Heard similar tales myself when I was in Poland. Utter bunkum!"

"Father thought so too," Ben told him. "But then he found something in the Warsaw Library which intrigued him. It was a passing reference in an old newspaper, to a visit made to Poland by an emissary of the Pope. Apparently, His Holiness wanted the rumours of lampirs to be investigated – so in 1830 the Vatican despatched a trusted priest called Father Tomasz Krystof."

"Never heard of him!" Sir Peter said dismissively.

"Neither had my father," Ben acknowledged. "But then he found out something rather odd. Soon after his investigations were complete, Father Tomasz Krystof renounced the priesthood and settled in a small village a few miles south of Warsaw. My father went there to interview him – and Father Tomasz's account of his investigations completely changed my father's mind about the plague, and about lampirs!"

"What do you mean?" Sir Peter demanded gruffly.

"During the early 1830s, Father Tomasz had travelled around Poland gathering stories and eyewitness accounts about lampir attacks. But on one occasion he became an eyewitness himself."

Sir Peter adjusted his monocle and frowned. "Go on. . ."

"The priest told my father that during the depths of winter, he arrived at the remote village of Osjec. It was late in the day, just before dusk, and the shadows were lengthening. People of all ages came pouring out of their houses to welcome him – men, women and children. They kissed the hem of his priestly robes and begged him to bless them. A white-haired old man explained to Father Tomasz that the local priest had died of a mysterious illness just the week before – the villagers were afraid for their mortal souls. . ."

Ben could see that he was drawing Sir Peter in with his tale. The historian had stopped stroking his dogs and was listening attentively.

"Father Tomasz celebrated Mass for them," Ben continued. "But he noticed that as the twilight deepened, the congregation began to creep away. Soon the church was empty, except for the white-haired old man. Father Tomasz asked him where everybody had gone. The old man told him that not a soul would dare venture on to the streets after dark, for fear that they would fall victim to the 'walking dead'. . ."

Across the sitting room, candles guttered, and the curtains stirred as if caught by a draught or a ghostly hand. Ben saw Emily glance nervously at the corners of the room and stifled a grin. Even she was uneasy, and she *knew* his story wasn't true.

He let his voice sink almost to a whisper for the next part of his tale. "Father Tomasz said that he was not afraid because the power of the Cross would protect him. He asked the old man to show him proof that the dead could walk, so the old man led him out into the shadowy churchyard and they hid themselves behind a gravestone. Together they waited . . . and they waited . . . while all around them the night grew colder, the sky grew darker, and the shadows grew blacker. Scudding clouds made strange shapes flicker across the frozen grass, but then Father Tomasz heard a sound, and the old man pointed a shaking finger. Across the churchyard, a grave was breaking open to let something out – something that could toss aside great clods of frozen earth as if they were handfuls of dust! Finally, the thing heaved itself out of the grave, and Father Tomasz realized that it was a dead man – its flesh rotting on its bones. . ." Ben leant a little further forward as if he was imparting a great secret. "It was a lampir!" he whispered.

And, at that, little Minty gave a low growl, the wind whistled at the windows, and all the candles on one side of the room went out.

Plunged into semi-darkness, Emily sat bolt upright, her heart pounding and her skin crawling with fear. Then she shook her head. Of course, it was *Ben* – he'd set the whole thing up! He'd chosen this wonderfully spooky black and purple room, lit the candles, left a window open somewhere and hoped that a gust of wind would extinguish the flames at some point during his tale. She grinned behind her hand and looked across at him. He was really very clever!

Sir Peter was also sitting bolt upright, staring at the dead candles. His monocled eye following the narrow, curling plumes of smoke that twisted upwards from the wicks. There was a moment of silence, then a log slipped in the grate and Sir Peter sat back, blinking.

"Go on, Benedict my boy," he said, smoothing Minty's tiny hackles down. "I'll hear you out. Still think it's bunkum, mind you. . ." But Emily could hear a note of doubt in his voice as he said it.

Ben glanced over his shoulder, his gaze darting to the shadows on the other side of the room. He's such a good actor, Emily thought. Anyone would think he was scared, too.

At last Ben seemed ready to carry on. He turned back to Sir Peter. "Father Tomasz told my father that he'd encountered many frightening things during his life as a priest, but the noise that the lampir made was the most terrifying sound he had ever heard. It was a deep, guttural groan, like a death rattle, that seemed to echo across the deserted graveyard."

"Ahem." Sir Peter coughed. "Death rattle, eh?"

Ben nodded. "Father Tomasz and the old man were rigid with fear as they watched the monster lurch towards the churchyard fence. Then the moon came out from behind a cloud. The creature seemed to ripple in the darkness, and then, all at once – it vanished!"

"Vanished?" Sir Peter sat forward, frowning slightly.

Emily could see that, almost against his will, the historian was being sucked into Ben's tale. "What do you mean – vanished?" he demanded.

"The old man told Father Tomasz that in the moonlight a lampir can adopt a shadow-form. Then it can slip across the ground, almost unnoticed, until it reaches its target – whereupon it rises up, solid once more, and devours the unsuspecting victim."

Sir Peter shifted in his seat. "And Harrison Cole believed all this?"

"He did." Ben nodded. "He said that Father Tomasz was the most convincing witness he had ever come across."

"Then why didn't the Vatican take action?"

"That's exactly what my father wanted to know," Ben replied. "Father Tomasz said simply that the Vatican didn't believe him – or they were too afraid to admit the truth! Officials told him to forget everything he'd seen, and to destroy all his writings. They threatened to excommunicate him if he ever breathed a word of what he had witnessed. That's why he renounced the priesthood. But he never forgot, and he carried on, privately, with his investigations."

Sir Peter's eyes bulged slightly and Emily hid a smile. This was working even better than they had hoped. Ben was so convincing – what would he come up with next?

"The priest told my father everything he had learned about lampirs – that they walk only in darkness, that daylight forces them into their shadow-form, that they have the strength of ten men. . ." Ben continued.

"T-ten men?" Sir Peter repeated hoarsely, and Emily could see that he was remembering the savage attack on the safe at the Royal Institution.

"Father Tomasz said that the only weapon which could defeat a lampir was the Dhampir Bell. But using that was dangerous, because the bell itself holds a certain fascination for the lampirs. It draws them. They will walk to the ends of the earth to find it."

"Find it?" echoed Sir Peter. He clutched Priss and Minty tightly to his chest and glanced up at the ceiling, as if he could see through the building to the Long Gallery and the Dhampir Bell.

"Indeed," Ben murmured. "Imagine the danger of keeping something here at Brayleigh Court which attracts lampirs so irresistibly. . ."

"N-nonsense," said Sir Peter, but he didn't sound very sure. "Lampirs? Here at Brayleigh Court? What a load of—"

But he broke off in mid-sentence, because at that moment, the curtains at the window billowed and an eerie growling sound was carried in on the night air. Barely audible at first, it gradually grew louder and louder, a rasping, unnatural groan – the death rattle of a lampir.

Sir Peter stared at Ben in horror. So did Emily – and her brother's white, shocked face told her all she needed to know.

Whatever Ben had done with the candles, he hadn't set *this* up. This was real!

CHAPTER TWENTY

Emily leapt to her feet and rushed to the window. Ben was right behind her, almost tripping over a frantic Priss and Minty in his haste.

"Er, ahem, very strange noise that!" Sir Peter said gruffly. Clearing his throat nervously, he crossed the room and clutched at Ben's arm.

Ben shook him off. Together he and Emily reached for the curtains and tore them aside, pressing their faces to the windowpane. It took a moment for their eyes to adjust to the darkness outside, but then – to their horror – they saw two shapes at the far end of the terrace, black silhouettes against the white stone balustrade.

Emily immediately saw that one was a hulking figure with clawed hands, its white face almost luminous in the moonlight, its terrifying death rattle echoing across the terrace.

"Good lord!" exclaimed Sir Peter. "Look at that!"

"It's a lampir," Ben gasped. "Quick – we need fire!"

Emily heard Sir Peter make a choking sound. "There are two of them," he moaned. "And each with the strength of ten men. Look! Look at the other one!"

Emily looked, and gave a startled gasp. "That's no 'other one'," she cried frantically. "That's Jack! He's being attacked by a lampir. Oh, what shall we do?" She pounded her fists helplessly against the glass of the window. "Stop! Leave him alone!"

The lampir's clawed hands swiped the air next to Jack's face. Jack leapt backwards, tripped over, and fell. He kicked his feet out at the lampir and tried to scramble away across the terrace. But the lampir kept coming. It was trying to bite Jack on the arm, the hand, the shoulder – anywhere.

Jack's cries of terror were muffled by the heavy French windows. "Help!" Jack flung his arm up across his face, trying to shield himself as the lampir raked his hair.

"We have to help him," Emily cried, struggling to open the window.

"I know!" Ben replied. He was already darting towards the doors that led out on to the terrace. "The lampir must have been drawn here by the Dhampir Bell," he cried, fumbling with the lock. "Let's hope there aren't more of them."

"More of them?" Sir Peter muttered, clearly terrified. "Right! I'll just go and, er . . . get my, er . . . my *gun*! Yes, that's it. I'll go and find my gun!" And he rushed from the room with Priss and Minty yapping at his heels.

Emily shoved hard on the sash window and it flew upwards at exactly the same moment that Ben managed to unlock the French windows. Together they burst out on to the terrace to help Jack.

But Jack didn't need their help. He was sitting up, grinning widely at them. And the lampir was standing up straight, too, its hands on its hips in a most un-lampir-like stance.

"What?" Ben exclaimed, doing a double-take.

Jack waved and gave them a thumbs-up sign. The lampir grinned, and held its thumbs up too.

"It's a trick!" Emily cried. "That's not a lampir – it's Filip."

"I'm going to kill them," Ben muttered, half-laughing with relief as Jack and Filip Cinska scrambled down the terrace steps and hared away towards the trees.

"Later," Emily said firmly, grasping his sleeve. "First we have to go and find Sir Peter."

After a hurried search, they finally found the historian in his bedroom. He emerged from behind a pink brocade armchair just as Ben and Emily knocked and came in.

"Sir Peter, are you all right?" Ben asked.

"Of course I'm jolly well all right," Sir Peter blustered. "I was just looking for my gun!" He aimed a light kick at the leg of the pink armchair. "This darn thing tripped me up. Yes, that's it! I tripped over, and fell down behind the chair. . . My only thought was to protect the two of you. . ."

But Emily knew that he'd been hiding. The historian looked very dishevelled and agitated. She exchanged a knowing look with Ben.

Sir Peter gave a little cough. "Er, has the creature gone?"

Ben nodded, and Sir Peter coughed again. "Naturally I would have dealt with it myself if I'd been able to stay," he said, beginning to smooth his hair back into place. "But, Benedict, dear boy, I've been thinking about the Dhampir Bell. I, er, I've decided that it might be a good idea to send it back to London. And perhaps offer it to the Polish Embassy or something. . ." He fiddled with his monocle for a moment. "Naturally, I would take it myself, but unfortunately, I have responsibilities here at Brayleigh Court. . ."

Sir Peter hesitated, and then looked directly at Ben. "Would you. . .? Could you. . .? *Might* you, Benedict, my boy – and your dear sister of course –" the historian bobbed his head vaguely in Emily's direction – "see your way to taking it with you tomorrow? First thing in the morning?"

CHAPTER TWENTY-ONE

"So in the end he gave it to you, just like that?" Feeling relieved, Jack sat back in the compartment of the Great Western train bound for London.

"Only because of you and Filip," Ben told him. "You were the ones that made him see sense. Not me!"

"Yes, you were brilliant," Emily said warmly. She was sitting in the far corner of the compartment by the window. Behind her a scene of bare, frost-tipped fields flashed by.

On her lap was the big blue hat-box, and Emily hugged it to her as if it contained the most precious hat in the world. But Jack knew that there was no hat in there. Nestled in soft folds of white silk was the Dhampir Bell.

Ben was sitting opposite his sister, his face flushed with the success of their mission. Filip Cinska was next to him, his hair back to its normal tousled state and his elbows poking through a new set of holes in his dusty old tailcoat.

"Looks like we owe you a new coat, Filip," Jack said.

Filip shrugged. "Me, I set no store by appearance. As long as clothing will keep me warm, then I am happy."

"How did you get the holes?" Emily asked.

"I tore ze coat when I climbed through ze gap in Sir Peter's hedge," Filip explained, tugging at his sleeve to inspect the damage. "Bare twigs, many thorns. . ." He winced. "Is nasty."

"So that's how you got in to Brayleigh Court," Ben said. "I lay awake wondering about it all last night. I knew the gates were locked, and I just couldn't work out how anyone might have got into the grounds."

Jack smiled. "Since when has a ten-foot wall kept *me* out?"

"I want to know about the candles," Emily said eagerly. "How did you get them to blow out?"

Ben raised his eyebrows. "I thought *you'd* arranged that, Em!"

"No," she laughed, shaking her head. "I thought *you* had."

"That was me," Jack put in. "But it was an accident. That small window was already open a crack, and I could hear you all in there, quite clearly – so I thought you could hear us. But Filip and I were out there fighting and making the death rattle for *ages*. Acting our hearts out, we were. But nobody heard us! So I had to sneak over and open the window a bit wider."

He grinned at the astonished looks on Ben and Emily's faces.

"What I'm curious about," Ben said, once he'd recovered from his surprise, "is how on earth Filip managed to be such a convincing lampir? I mean – that death rattle was superb! And the white face – it seemed to glow in the dark!"

"Death rattle is easy!" Filip declared. "Remember? All I need is a good cup of strong Polish tea!"

Everyone laughed at that.

"And the white face?" Emily prompted.

Filip grinned and delved into his pocket. He drew out a handful of small lacquered pots, the lids painted with Eastern European motifs: bluebirds, flowers, tiny curling vines. Inside the first one was a small grey sponge and a hard cake of something silvery-white.

"Make-up," Filip explained. "Mixture of rosewater and alum powders and zinc. You make it wet and spread on thickly. It covers ze face and neck to make you look like a ghost! I used a black one too, for dark shadows under ze eyes."

They all looked with interest at the little pots of vermilion paste, charcoal, and blue-tinted paint that Cinska carried in his seemingly bottomless pockets.

"You were a brilliant lampir," Emily said in an awed voice.

"Yes, you certainly had me convinced!" Ben agreed.

Jack grinned. "Go on, Filip, tell them," he urged.

164

Cinska looked bashful. "Well . . . all right," he said at last. "We are friends, so I tell you. In Poland, I used to work in a theatre troupe. We travelled around all of Eastern Europe performing music shows and miming. I am good at playing a funny clown, and a hunch-backed man – and sometimes I am your old Queen Elizabeth, with a white face and a big red-hair wig."

Ben and Emily dissolved into laughter. Jack chuckled too, feeling a strange kind of release. The sensation was a welcome one after the days of dark tension since their first sight of a lampir in the cemetery.

Before they knew it, the train was pulling in to Paddington Station in a cloud of steam and sooty smuts. People crowded the platforms, busy with their luggage. Somewhere a news-boy shouted, "*London Gazette* – get the latest!"

A short journey by hackney coach took the four friends and their luggage south-east across the city to Waterloo Bridge. There they said goodbye to Filip, who said he would make his own way back across the river to Tiler's Alley. Then it was home to Bedford Square.

Mrs Mills opened the door, beaming with pleasure. "You're back early!" she exclaimed. "Bless me, it's almost as if you knew you had a visitor!"

"A visitor?" Ben shrugged off his overcoat.

"Down in the kitchens," Mrs Mills said, and held the

door open as all three of them hurried down the steps to the servants' quarters.

Little Henry was sitting on the huge kitchen table, swinging his feet and munching a chunk of bread covered in thick butter and homemade plum jam.

Cook was standing beside him with her hands on her ample hips, smiling broadly with approval. "Boy's got an appetite," she said, bustling away across the kitchen to gather up baking tins and bags of flour. "I'll have to bake another loaf if you're all thinking of tucking in, too."

Ben grinned. "Well, now you mention it. . ." he said, and helped himself to a slice of bread and jam.

Standing with the big blue hat-box propped under her chin, Emily smiled at the sight of little Henry. "Good morning," she said. "Glad to see you're wearing my red scarf."

"Oh, it's a lifesaver," Henry replied around a mouthful of bread and jam. "Keeps me so warm I even wears it in bed at night!"

"I'm pleased you came back to see us," Ben told him.

"Aha. . ." Henry swallowed his mouthful quickly. "Well, this ain't what you toffs – not meaning no disrespect, mind – but it ain't what you toffs would call a 'social call'."

Ben felt a tug of alarm. "What do you mean, Henry?"

"I've been noticing things," the little boy explained quietly. He glanced at Cook, but she was busy at the other end of the kitchen, weighing out flour and salt into an enormous glass bowl.

"What things?" Jack asked.

"A lot of people on the streets ain't looking quite right," Henry went on. "Couple o' families near where I live – they've been poorly for a few days. You know the sort of thing – aches and pains, sniffles, feeling cold. Nothing unusual for the time o' year." He glanced at Jack and added, "But, well, you remember Molly's gran? *She* was ill like that, not long ago, and *she* died. And then so did my Uncle Jerzy."

Jack nodded grimly.

Henry continued. "Well, yesterday I bumped into one of the lads on the landing and he told me how his grandad's fingernails've turned purple. And I remembered that that's what happened to Molly's gran and Uncle Jerzy, when they was first ill!"

Ben, Emily and Jack all exchanged worried looks.

"Go on," Ben told Henry.

"So I was thinking about these purple nails as I went downstairs. And when I went out into the lane I saw the old bloke who comes round collecting rags and rubbish. He was standing there by his push-cart, dabbing his nose. His fingernails were the most 'orrible colour you've ever seen."

"Purple," put in Emily.

Henry nodded. "I think it's spreading," he said. "Last night and this morning I've seen loads of sickly souls. All shivering and wiping their noses and staring at their fingernails. So I thought I'd come here. 'Go and tell yer old mate, Jack,' I says to meself. 'He'll know what to do.' " Henry looked anxious. "Is it a plague? Are we all going to die?"

There was an awkward silence. Jack swallowed hard and put his arm round the little lad's shoulders.

Then Cook came waddling across the kitchen with flour up to her elbows and a cross look on her face. "If you've all quite finished eating, I'll ask you to take your tales of plague and sickness right out of my kitchen! I don't want it cluttered up with a bunch of people muttering about *plague*!"

"Sorry," Ben said with a sheepish grin.

He led them all up to the drawing-room, where Henry goggled at the Christmas tree, which he'd been too scared to notice during the fight with his Uncle Jerzy. It was a good five minutes before any of them could get any sense out of him.

"This is more serious than we thought," Ben said to Jack and Emily. "If the plague is spreading this fast, then we have to move ahead with the plan. And the sooner the better."

"Nothing's stopping us, now that we've got the Dhampir Bell," Jack pointed out. He turned to Henry. "We're going to need your help."

Henry nodded, dragging his gaze away from the Christmas tree and concentrating on Jack. "Anything," he said.

Between them, Ben and Jack filled in the details for

Henry, telling him what they knew about lampirs and how to defeat them.

"It has to be fire, you see," Ben explained. "Nothing else will kill them. We need to lure them somewhere, a place where nobody else will get hurt, so that we can set fire to them and destroy them."

"You spend a lot of time around the docks, Henry," Jack said thoughtfully. "You know all the old warehouses and sheds – is there anywhere that's empty at the moment? A place no one uses no more?"

"That's a brilliant idea, Jack," Emily said. She was sitting in one of the over-stuffed armchairs, the blue hat-box on the floor beside her.

Henry thought for a moment, his brow furrowed. "Can't think of anywhere," he said at last. "There was an old wooden warehouse over on St Katherine's Docks that was empty for a few weeks. But it's full of China tea now." He sighed and poked at the carpet with the scuffed toe of his boot. Then abruptly his face brightened. "I know of a ship that's about to be broken up for salvage – will that do?"

Ben grinned widely. "It'll more than do. It'll be perfect!"

"You'd probably have to buy it," Henry said dubiously.

Ben puffed out his cheeks. "I could talk to our solicitor, see whether I can borrow some money from the Trust Fund my father set up before he went to Mexico. Henry, do you know who the ship belongs to?"

"Yeah." Henry nodded. "The captain's a Polish bloke called Aleksy Marek. He used to be a friend of Uncle Jerzy's. I'll go and see him, shall I? Arrange for you all to meet up and talk about a price."

"Good idea," Ben said. "Tell him it's urgent and ask if he'll see us today. Meanwhile, I'll go and talk to our solicitor, Mr Fothergill, about the money."

The two boys left immediately, leaving Jack and Emily to eat lunch alone. Neither one was hungry, and they both pushed their food around their plates in thoughtful silence.

Eventually Jack spoke hesitantly, "Do you remember a few days ago, Em, when I said maybe Molly had been run over trying to escape from a lampir? I reckon the lampir might have been her grandmother, hunting for the blood of a living relative."

Emily looked up from her meal and sat back. "Poor Molly! No wonder she ran out in the road without looking," she remarked sadly.

Neither of them felt much like eating after that, so they abandoned lunch and positioned themselves by the window of the drawing-room to wait for Ben and Henry to return. Emily sat in the window seat with her feet tucked up under her, and Jack slumped in one of the over-stuffed armchairs.

Finally Emily saw Ben walking towards the house. There was such a spring in his step that she guessed he'd been successful with Mr Fothergill.

Henry appeared next, not far behind Ben, calling "Hello" and running to catch up.

Moments later they both burst into the drawing-room, bringing with them a chilly blast of December air.

"Did it!" exclaimed Ben, beaming. He patted his coat pocket meaningfully, and Emily knew that meant he had the money.

"Me too!" chimed Henry, with a grin. "Captain Marek said to come now. He weren't so keen at first. But I made out you were gentlemen-buyers with cash to burn, and he perked up a bit then. I tells him he'd get more money for the ship if it was sold to you, than if it was just broken up for salvage. 'Nobody wants wooden sailing ships now,' I says to 'im, 'it's all steam boats and engines, ain't it?' And he agreed. Said he'd sell to you, but only if you hurry, 'cos he's got the salvage man coming first thing tomorrow morning."

Jack stood up. "Looks like we're just in time then," he said. He picked up the hat-box with the Dhampir Bell in it and glanced round at the others. "Shall we go?"

They flagged down a hackney carriage out on New Oxford Street. As it rattled towards their destination, Emily noticed that Ben had one of their father's frock coats over his arm. "Why have you brought that?" she asked.

"I thought we'd better collect Filip Cinska on the way," Ben explained. "Captain Marek won't want to hand over his ship to four children, no matter how much money we wave under his nose. We need a grown-up to make sure he takes us seriously."

"That's a good idea," Emily agreed. "The frock coat's for Filip, then?"

Ben nodded. "His old one's got holes all over it. I'm sure Father would want him to have this, and we need him to look respectable!"

The hackney dropped them at Tiler's Alley, where Filip Cinska was delighted with his new coat. Ben explained what they needed him to do and he was more than happy to accompany the friends on their mission. Then Henry led the way to the docks. The wharves were alive with the hustle and bustle of day's end. Sailors and dockhands hurried this way and that, passengers milled about several of the gangplanks, and shoreside lanterns began to wink into life as the lamplighter did his rounds.

Henry paused and looked around. The sun had dipped low in the sky. It was a crimson fireball that now dappled all the surrounding warehouses and ships with glowing shades of red and gold. He pointed to a lone merchant ship which was moored in a single berth at the far end of the wharf. The three-master looked as though it had weathered one storm too many: the paint on the hull was peeling badly and some of the yard-arms were broken.

Emily realized that it must be Captain Marek's ship.

"There she is," Henry declared proudly. "The *Polish Princess*. The captain said he'd be in the warehouse down the end there, busy with the cargo from his last trip. Come on, follow me."

It was a long walk to the far end of the wharf, and by the time they reached the enormous doors to the last warehouse, the sun was just sinking behind the tall buildings up-river. Tendrils of mist had begun to curl up from the dark surface of the Thames. There were only one or two lamps at this end of the docks, and all five of the friends glanced warily left and right. It was very quiet here. Emily tightened her hand on Jack's arm.

"We could do with a bit of light," Ben said. "Let me sort something out." He kicked around among the piles of timber and rope until he found a two-foot length of wood with a lick of tar at the end. Then he climbed up on to a packing crate and opened one of the nearby lamps. The flame flickered wildly in the chill evening air, but it was enough. Within moments Ben had a makeshift torch, its tarred end flaming cheerily in the dim light of the sunset.

"Right," Ben said. "I'll go first, then." He strode bravely towards the warehouse and pushed open the door. Inside, it was pitch black. He paused. "Henry, are you sure Captain Marek said he'd be here?"

Henry nodded. "He's staying until about ten o'clock tonight, filling in Excise forms for the harbourmaster."

"All right, then," Ben muttered.

Cautiously they made their way inside. The torch guttered and flared, giving just enough light for them to see by. There were tea chests and packing crates piled high all around the warehouse. Dead ahead a narrow pathway cut between two towering rows of boxes.

"Captain Marek?" Ben called.

He and Jack moved forward in the darkness, Ben holding the torch high. Emily felt Henry reach for her hand and she took his willingly, welcoming the comfort of human contact. Filip Cinska brought up the rear. The silence seemed to press in around them.

"There's nobody here," Emily said softly.

Henry's fingers tightened on hers. "But Captain Marek *said. . ."*

Ahead, Ben and Jack had emerged into what seemed to be a clearing in the middle of the warehouse. Ben raised the flaming torch and Emily looked upwards, following its plume of smoke. There were rafters high above, strung with thick cobwebs. Knotted ends of rope hung from one or two, as if pulleys had been used in the past.

Emily's attention was brought back to ground level by a sudden, sharp cry from Ben. He and Jack darted forward. They peered at something on the floor in front of them. As Ben held the torch out, the light fell on the dark shape of a man. He was stretched out on his back, with his arms flung wide. Clutched in one of his hands was a spent candle, which he'd obviously been using to light his way in the warehouse. He wore a heavy blue coat, with a red-spotted kerchief knotted around his neck. His black hair and beard contrasted sharply with the stark white of his skin.

But then Emily realized that the man wasn't naturally pale. He'd been drained of blood – and the red spots on the neckerchief were the last drops, spilled as a lampir tore the flesh from his throat. His clothes were in shreds, and as Emily drew closer, she saw that he'd been bitten all over, on his arms, legs and chest.

Emily gasped and Henry peeped out cautiously from behind her skirts.

Jack fell to his knees, placed the hat-box carefully on the floor beside him, and reached out a trembling hand. "This must be Captain Marek," he said hoarsely.

"It is! It is!" wailed Henry.

"Is he dead?" Emily asked flatly.

Ben sighed. "Yes," he replied. "The poor man's dead."

Filip approached the body and pulled the neckerchief away from the dead man's neck to inspect the wounds there. When he had finished, his face was grim. "The captain was Polish, yes?"

Henry nodded.

Filip sighed. "Then I would say that Marek's lampir relatives got to him before we did."

"But how?" Emily whispered. "It's only just sunset. I thought they couldn't take physical form during daylight hours?"

"Not in daylight, no," Filip agreed. "Even the slightest glimmer of daylight keeps them in shadow-form. But in here –" he waved an arm to take in the darkness of the warehouse – "here it is like night. The door is shut tight, the place is stacked full of crates. Captain Marek was working by the light of a candle because there was no natural light. The lampirs could easily take human-form in here."

There was a long silence as the little party took this in. Then Jack stood up. "There's nothing we can do for the captain. I think we'd better get out of here, before. . ."

His voice trailed off and Emily glanced up to see that Jack's face had become a mask of horror. She swallowed and turned slowly to peer over her shoulder, following Jack's gaze, which was fixed on the shadows rippling and thickening in the darkness beyond the circle of torchlight. Dozens of lampirs were closing in. They lurched forwards from behind the crates and packing cases, their eyeballs shining milky-white in the half-light, their claw-like hands reaching out towards the humans.

Too late, the friends realized they were surrounded.

CHAPTER TWENTY-TWO

"Everybody get behind me!" Ben hissed urgently, brandishing the flaming torch in front of him. "They're afraid of fire, remember?"

"There's so many of them," Henry said in a terrified voice. "Where'd they all come from?"

"They've been here the whole time," Filip replied grimly. "Watching from the shadows."

The friends drew close together, forming a tight cluster. Then Ben advanced, waving the torch ahead of him. It was very effective. Some of the lampirs cowered away, their greeny-white eyeballs rolling, their lips peeling back from their fangs in angry snarls. But it wasn't enough, and Ben knew it. The friends were completely surrounded. However much Ben swung the torch, he knew he could only cover part of the group. Jack and Filip, at the rear, were defenceless, exposed.

"The candle," Ben muttered. "Jack, can you get the candle?"

Jack dived forwards, snatched the candle from Captain Marek's dead hand, and lit the wick from Ben's torch.

"It's such a small flame!" Emily wailed.

"Better than nothing," Jack said doggedly. "And it'll have to do. Those rags the lampirs are wearing look pretty dry. They should go up in flames if the creatures get too near. It'll only take one of 'em to burn for all of them to realize that even a candle can be lethal to their sort."

To prove his point, Jack jabbed the candle sharply to his left where a lampir had come in close. It was a woman, the remnants of a green gown hanging from her half-rotten flesh. Jack's candle caught the lace around one cuff. The fabric crackled for a moment, then burst into flame.

There was a horrible sound as the lampir-woman shrieked and twisted away, agony etched across her ravaged face. Flames ran up her arms and set her bodice alight. For a moment she looked like a candle herself, then fire engulfed her. She turned greyish-black, kept her shape for an instant, then collapsed inwards in a pile of gritty, grey ash.

"Good one, Jack," Ben said. But as the words left his mouth he realized it was not good. Not good at all. Far from making the lampirs afraid, Jack's action seemed to have made them angry. They growled ominously and a few ran forwards, into the group.

Ben caught a glimpse of a boy not much older than himself, newly-dead by the look of his perfect, waxy skin. But he didn't stop to think about what the boy might have been. He waved the torch at him with one hand, and landed a hard punch with the other – right on the boy's nose. Instantly the lampir melted into shadow-form and slid away across the floor.

Beside him, Jack was doing battle with another lampir, punching and kicking until it too slipped into shadow-form. But no sooner had that one gone than another took its place; a huge man, taller than the rest and long-dead, with stringy muscles holding his jaws shut.

Filip let out a roar and rushed forwards, his fist catching the tall lampir-man in the middle of his chest. For an instant, grey ribs showed through the ragged strips of his shirt, then he was gone – a shadow rippling away across the floor. But the lampir was immediately replaced by another, and another, and yet another.

"We've got to get out of here," Jack gasped. "There's too many for us to be able to fight them in physical form. We need the daylight."

"By now it's probably dark outside, too," Ben reminded him.

"Well, at least we'll have a chance to get away," Jack argued. "We can hold them off while the others make a run for it."

Ben saw the sense in that. "All right," he agreed. "Everybody stay together. Back to back. I know it's hard, but try to make sure the torch and the candle are between you and the lampirs."

They began to move, slowly inching their way towards the entrance to the warehouse. Lampirs crowded round, growling, their faces twisted in hunger and bloodlust. One of them lunged forwards, snapping at Emily's face. She jumped back just in time, and then Jack was there, somehow driving the lampir back with his meagre candle flame.

Shadows flickered everywhere – on the packing crates, up the walls, across the floor and ceiling. One lampir came rippling beneath their feet and began to rematerialize right in their midst, but Ben was ready for it. As Emily and the others leapt away, he jabbed the torch at the lampir's stomach and it went up in a blaze of golden flame.

Too late, Ben realized that though the lampir was gone, it had achieved its aim – it had split the group. He, Jack and Emily were one side of the pile of cinders and ash, Filip and Henry were the other.

Another lampir rose up in the middle of the group. It solidified, but Jack was there in time, attacking with the candle.

"Filip!" Ben shouted. "Henry!" He could see that they had become separated from each other. Henry was darting nimbly between two lampirs, as if he was trying to reach the door. Meanwhile, Filip was fighting a lampir who only seemed to have one arm. Then Ben realized that Filip had torn off the lampir's other arm and was using it as a club, beating the lampir around the head and neck with it. The hand flexed with life, but Cinska was oblivious in his grim determination. He held on tight and kept on fighting.

The lampir staggered under the fury of Filip's onslaught. Filip took advantage of the brief respite to dive towards Ben, thrusting the dead arm towards the torch and gasping, "Light it!"

Ben did so quickly, and soon Filip, too, had a torch – albeit a grisly one, with a thick jacket sleeve still in place around it and the hand opening and closing with independent life.

But it was an effective weapon, because as Filip twirled the makeshift torch around his head, all the lampirs cowered back, groaning and growling, their breath hissing angrily through their fangs.

"The door!" Filip shouted. "Get to the door!"

He pointed and Ben saw that they were nearer than he'd realized. The door was only a few feet away. Just two lampirs stood between him and their escape. Ben lunged with his torch, yelling wildly and dragging Emily with him. Together they threw themselves against the door and it flew open, letting the last rays of reddened sunlight into the warehouse. The lampirs caught in the daylight turned instantly to shadow.

Ben and Emily hovered, safe, in the doorway, desperately looking for their friends. A moment later,

Filip came running out of the darkness still clutching the burning lampir-arm. And Jack appeared too, the hat-box clutched under one arm and the candle held high over his head.

"Come on!" Jack gasped. They all dashed outside just as the sunset disappeared and darkness closed around them.

"But Henry. . ." Ben felt his heart lurch painfully. *"Where's Henry?"*

He wasn't there. With a yell, Jack made as if to dash back into the warehouse, but Ben grasped his sleeve. "Wait," he said. "It's too dangerous, and you've only got a candle. I'll go."

Jack's expression was grim. He tossed the candle on to the ground and grabbed Filip's burning lampir-arm. "We'll both go," he said firmly.

But as they started forwards, a wall of shadows came surging out of the warehouse doorway towards them, the lampirs gradually rematerializing into solid human-form now that night had fallen. Ben counted six . . . ten . . . *twenty* of them. . .

Too many to fight. Too many to hope that Henry was still alive.

The friends staggered backwards under the onslaught, and Jack screamed, *"NO!"*

CHAPTER TWENTY-THREE

"Right, that's it," Jack snapped. He was so angry at losing Henry that he could barely speak. "We're going to finish these lampirs once and for all!"

He thrust the lampir-arm at Filip, who gripped it hard and turned to face the enemy, waving his grisly torch at the advancing lampirs.

But the thick jacket that surrounded the arm had burned through and the lampir-flesh caught fire. Instantly it flared, bright orange. The next moment, Filip was holding nothing but a handful of ash. Disgusted, he flung it to the floor.

Meanwhile, Jack had placed the hat-box on the ground and was prising off the lid. He lifted out the Dhampir Bell.

"Let me help you, Jack," Ben said, and passed his torch to Emily, who stood shoulder-to-shoulder with Filip, wielding the flaming length of wood like a sword.

Together Jack and Ben held the Dhampir Bell up high

and let the clapper swing. The chime echoed out in waves, melodious and beautiful. Jack thought he'd never heard such a wonderful sound in his life before. It was hypnotic . . .

He shook himself. *Not you, fool*, he thought sternly. *It's the lampirs who are supposed to be mesmerized!*

And they were. Jack could see them by the light of the torch, their faces rapt. Some were drooling, while others crooned in an eerie, sing-song wail. A few of them stopped in their tracks and began to sway, their blind, milky-white eyes rolling towards the night sky.

Jack and Ben began to back away. "Come on," Jack muttered. "Come this way."

Emily and Filip backed away too, as the lampirs came forward in a wave, surging out of the warehouse and fanning out across the wharf. Grey mist swirled around their feet. One or two of them seemed to be recovering from their mesmerized state. They slashed their clawed hands at the friends, eager to take hold of the bell. A few slipped into shadow-form in the light from the torch and Jack felt a jolt of panic. *Not shadow-form!* he thought. He knew they could fight the lampirs as humans, but battling shadows was impossible. He nodded to Ben and they rang the bell again.

Immediately the lampirs swooned, groaning softly.

"Let's get to Captain Marek's ship," Ben said urgently. "Let's draw them there, and finish them off. Just like we planned."

Together they turned to run in the direction of the ship, Jack with the Dhampir Bell cradled in his arms. But the sight that met their eyes was terrifying. A great wave of movement rolled towards them out of the thickening mist. Lampirs! Hundreds of them. Some in human-form. Some as shadows. Men, women, small children – all dead, all with clawed hands, milky eyeballs and vicious fangs.

They were coming from the city, clawing their way out of their graves to follow the sound of the Dhampir Bell through London's fog-bound streets.

Jack shook his head to clear it. "Run! To the ship!" he yelled.

The *Polish Princess* was swathed in mist, her masts and cross-trees skeletal against the gloom. The lampirs were advancing down the wharf, but there was still time to get to the ship – or was there? Jack saw with a jolt that one or two lampirs were running towards him with a strange, lop-sided gait. They came close, groaning, their clawed hands snatching at the bell.

Jack ducked and weaved. But they were fast. And strong. One of them seized the rim of the Dhampir Bell and tugged. . .

But suddenly, Ben was there, landing deft, hard punches on the side of the lampir's head. And Emily stabbed at it with the torch until it burst into flames. They all leapt backwards, and Jack could feel the heat on his face as the lampir burned. It was gone, but there were more in its wake, lurching towards Jack and reaching for the bell.

Jack ran on towards the *Polish Princess*. He heard Filip shout, "We are almost at the gangplank. Mind your footing. Don't trip over!"

Jack felt sideways with his feet as Emily kept the lampirs back. Then he felt it – Filip was right, they were at the gangplank. He could feel the slope. Then he was edging up to board the ship. He glanced back and saw Filip and Ben right behind him. Ben was holding Emily round the waist, keeping her moving even as she fended off the lampirs with the torch.

Clutching the bell tightly, Jack clambered on board the *Polish Princess*. "The prow," he gasped. "Let's get up to the prow, it's the furthest point. . ." And he hurried across the wooden deck, sidestepping coils of rope and folds of canvas sailcloth. The others were right behind him. A breeze rippled through the rigging high above Jack's head. It made the ropes thrum. The buckles and blocks began to clank.

Then Filip's voice rose above the clamour. "They are coming! They are coming!" he cried.

Dozens of lampirs swarmed up the gangplank, their lips drawn back from their glistening fangs. Behind them, Jack could see more – many more – streaming along the dockside, melting into shadow-form as they moved through puddles of lamplight. And beyond them, he knew with a terrified certainty, there were hundreds of others pouring in from the streets and alleys of night-time London.

"We haf to get them all on board," he said to Ben.

Ben nodded, his face terrified but determined. "I didn't realize there would be so many," he said hoarsely. "This plague. . ."

But there was no time to think about the plague. Reaching the prow at last, Jack rang the Dhampir Bell again. The mesmerizing chime echoed through the foggy night, reverberating against the walls of the warehouses.

"Look out!" yelled Filip. A lampir – a hulking man with fangs the size of knife-blades – lurched towards the prow of the ship. He was so close that Jack could smell his putrefying flesh. He lunged at Jack, and Jack leapt away, holding the Dhampir Bell close. But he was trapped, his back against a wooden rail.

Clumsily, the lampir made a grab for the bell. And Ben hurled himself forwards, knocking into the lampir and sending it flying across the deck. The lampir staggered against the side-rail, lost its balance and fell overboard with a loud splash.

The boys rushed to peer over the side of the ship. "There it is!" Jack cried. "It's trying to climb up one of the ropes."

"Then it will get burned when the ship goes up," Ben replied grimly. He looked at his sister. "It's time, Emily! Start setting fire to the boat!" he shouted.

Emily darted forwards, dodging lampirs who staggered

away at the sight of her flaming torch. There wasn't much left of the torch now – just a few inches of blackened wood – but she quickly touched it to the piles of canvas sailcloth and coils of tar-coated rope. They went up in spectacular flames, crackling and spitting. The tar softened, melted and trickled across the deck, carrying the bright flames. The slight breeze fanned the fire, driving it higher and higher.

Her face a mask of determination, Emily moved methodically from the port side of the ship to the starboard, setting fire to everything in her path: ropes, folded sails, wooden barrels and casks.

Soon a barrier of raging fire separated the prow of the ship from the main deck. Black smoke rose in plumes. Beyond it Jack could see scores of lampirs swarming across the decks. One or two lampirs had become trapped this side of the fiery barrier, but Filip and Ben finished them off by pushing them hard into the flames. The lampirs went up like fireworks, flaring orange and crimson.

Jack could feel the heat on his face now. The smoke stung his eyes. He flung one arm up, clutching the Dhampir Bell tightly. His movement made the clapper strike the side of the bell yet again. The sound of the beautiful chime rose above the roar of the fire. Several lampirs sighed and moaned, as if driven half-mad by the knowledge that the bell was so close, but out of reach. A few of them threw themselves forwards across the barrier of flames, but were incinerated before they reached Jack and the bell.

But then Jack heard a sound behind him. A rasping, triumphant cry. He twisted round in time to see that lampirs were swarming up the lines which secured the *Polish Princess* to her mooring. Drawn by the sound of the bell, they were clambering over the side-rails to come aboard.

Emily saw them at almost the same moment as Jack and she was at his side in an instant, touching the last of her torch to the anchor-lines. The ropes burnt and frayed, then fell away. But it was too late. A dozen lampirs had already clambered aboard this way and were now closing in on the friends – or, more specifically, Jack realized, on him and the Dhampir Bell.

Jack looked around wildly for some means of escape – but this time he could see nowhere to run.

CHAPTER TWENTY-FOUR

His mind racing, Jack glanced upwards. *There has to be some way out*, he thought. An idea struck him. "There's nowhere to go but up!" he yelled to the others. "We have to climb the rigging!"

Climbing one-handed, with the Dhampir Bell tucked against his side, was hard work. Jack hauled himself up the lines, using the cross-ropes as steps. Filip Cinska was right beside him, helping Jack climb by grabbing his collar and taking some of his weight. Jack could barely breathe now; the smoke was thick and black, stinging his eyes, his nose, his lungs. . .

As he climbed, Jack saw that the water below was rippling and the masts of the ship were swaying. All at once it dawned on him that when the mooring ropes had burned through, the ship had begun to drift out into the river. He looked down. Emily was below and to his left, climbing steadily with Ben just below her.

But Jack saw something else. Something that made his

blood freeze. "Look out!" he shouted. "The lampirs are on their way!"

And they were, shinning up the ropes and snatching at Ben's feet. Ben kicked out, smashing his boot against a lampir's hand and sending the creature spinning down to the burning deck below. But no sooner had he knocked back one, than another took its place.

Flames followed the lampirs, flickering along the ropes, racing up the lines and spreading out along the cross-trees. The whole ship was an inferno now, drifting out into the middle of the river with only its three masts standing clear of the flames.

Ben kicked down hard at another lampir. It fell away with a howl and Ben continued to climb steadfastly upwards. Then he realized he couldn't climb any further. His cheek was pressed against Emily's boot and her petticoats were frothing around his head.

"What is it?" he said. His voice cracked as he spoke. The heat from the fire had parched his throat and seared his lips. "Em, why have you stopped?"

"We're at the top," Emily replied. "There's nowhere else to go."

Jack's voice reached Ben from above, drifting down through the clouds of smoke that billowed around them. "Listen," he gasped. "We're going to have to jump, all right? We'll throw ourselves clear."

"But if we jump, then the lampirs will jump too," Ben protested.

"Not if we time it right," Jack shouted back. "They're in much more danger than us because they catch fire so easily. If we can hang on until the very last minute – when most of them are burning – we should still be able to jump free."

"All right," Ben agreed.

"Emily? Filip?" Jack called.

"Agreed!" they both chimed.

So the four friends waited. And watched.

Far below, Ben could see lampirs on fire, staggering across the main deck, or stumbling around in the prow of the ship. Nearly all of them were on board now, just a few stragglers remained on the dockside. They'd arrived too late to get on to the ship, but the bell had such a powerful draw that they were throwing themselves into the river to try and reach it.

Crack!

A new sound joined the roar of the fire and the groaning of the lampirs.

Creak . . . crack!

"The masts!" Jack shouted desperately. "Look – one of them's coming down!"

At the far end of the ship, the smallest of the three masts had burned through at its base. It was leaning at an angle now, held in place only by the rigging. But all the ropes and lines were quickly burning through. Even as Ben watched, they snapped under the weight of the mast and began to flail through the air like fiery whips.

Crash! As the ropes gave way, the mast spiralled downwards and hit the deck with such force that a huge plume of smoke and sparks exploded into the night air.

"We have to jump *now*!" Emily cried. "Jack?"

Jack nodded. "You and Ben go first," he gasped. "Filip and I will follow. Agreed?"

Filip was still holding tight to Jack's collar, helping to hold him up. "Agreed, my friend," he said.

Ben caught Jack's eye briefly and they exchanged a nod. "See you on shore," Ben said.

Jack watched Ben and Emily leap away from the top of the mast. Emily's petticoats billowed out around her . . . then, SPLASH! They hit the water holding hands. There was a moment of nothing – just the black surface of the Thames curling with tendrils of mist. Jack scanned the water frantically. *Where are they?* he wondered.

At last two heads bobbed up, one fair and one reddish-brown. There was a flurry of small splashes as Ben and Emily struck out for the shore. Jack sighed with relief; they were safe.

Then he realized that he could feel the heat of the flames licking at the soles of his boots. He turned to Filip. "Ready?"

They braced themselves, but abruptly Filip twisted on his piece of rigging and gasped, "Wait! There is something we must do." He looped his arm through the rigging and reached inside the Dhampir Bell. One tug, a deft twist, and he had broken the clapper off its yoke.

"This bell must not be rung again until it can be used to trap ze lampirs in their graves," Filip said, his face stern. He held the clapper high above his head. Jack saw it glinting in the firelight – one moment bronze, the next deepest crimson. Then Filip cast it down on to the burning deck, far below where it was immediately swallowed up by the flames.

"Now, jump!" Filip cried.

Jack jumped, the bell cradled against his chest. The fall seemed to go on for ever. He had an impression of heat, and light, and caught a glimpse of the burning lampirs on the decks of the *Polish Princess* as he fell past. Then he hit the water with a sharp smack – and sank like a stone.

Jack felt the water close over his head. Everything was black, silent and icy cold. He couldn't see a thing. He kicked out hard with both feet, but it was no good. He was sinking. The Dhampir Bell was so heavy it was weighing him down! He struggled in the depths of the murky water, unwilling to let go of the bell. There was a roaring in his ears. Silver spots danced before his eyes. His lungs burnt and he knew he'd have to breathe soon.

Then he felt someone grasp his arm and haul him upwards. His head broke the water and he gasped, dragging air into his tortured lungs as Filip's voice filtered into his consciousness. . .

"Steady, my friend. Breathe. Breathe. And do not drop ze bell!"

CHAPTER TWENTY-FIVE

Back on dry land at last, Emily staggered to a nearby bollard and sat down heavily. Bits of smouldering timber littered the ground around her. She realized they must have fallen off the *Polish Princess* when it was still at its mooring. She was soaked to the skin, her hair plastered to her head, her petticoats sodden and heavy. And her hands – *Why do they hurt so much?* she wondered.

She uncurled her fingers and stared down at her palms. They were bright red, blistered where she'd clung to the flaming torch even as it burned away to nothing.

Ben was bent double beside her, coughing the river water from his lungs. "I've heard the Thames is filthy," he gasped, his eyes watery. "But I didn't realize quite how bad it was. We're going to stink for days!"

Filip and Jack were flopped on the walkway by the edge of the wharf, flat on their backs, breathing heavily. A puddle spread out from their sopping clothes. Jack still had the Dhampir Bell clutched in the curve of his arm.

He raised his head and stared out across the river. "Look at that," he murmured.

They all looked. The night sky was lit with an orange glow that turned the surface of the water to molten gold. The burning *Polish Princess* was adrift in the middle of the Thames, half swathed in mist. All her masts were down now, and there wasn't much left of the hull. There was a popping sound, then the boom of an explosion deep in the hold. Soon there would just be a few charred timbers, floating down-river.

"It's a good job the tide is taking her away from the other ships," Ben remarked. "It'd be terrible if the fire spread."

Emily shivered, her teeth chattering, and Ben put his sodden jacket around her shoulders. She could feel something heavy in one of the pockets, and fished out a pouch of coins.

"The money!" she exclaimed. "We were going to give this to Captain Marck."

The excitement of the afternoon seemed such a long time ago. So much had happened since Ben had returned from seeing the solicitor. They had found the captain's dead body, fought the lampirs, lost poor little Henry, and finally set fire to the *Polish Princess*.

Tears pricked Emily's eyelids at the memory of Henry. She gazed out at the burning ship. "Do you think any of the lampirs survived?" she asked.

Filip sat up. "They could not haf survived such an inferno," he said, his voice full of relief.

"We've done it, then," Ben said, flatly. "I can hardly believe it's over."

"We haf indeed 'done it'," Filip agreed. "But we must celebrate our victory in some other place, or we will be bombarded with questions that we cannot answer. Look!"

At the far end of the wharf, dockers were running back and forth, panicked by the fire. Some shouted instructions, others fetched buckets in case the fire spread. Warehouse doors were dragged open and lamps shone in the foggy darkness. A bell began to clang, its warning clamour echoing across the river.

"Come away quickly," Filip urged. "We must not be seen here."

The friends scrambled to their feet, hurrying for the shadows. But then they heard halting footsteps approaching and, out of nowhere, an enormous lampir lurched towards them. It was clearly lame and had arrived at the docks too late to board the ship. Now its devilish face was suffused with rage. Its skin was stretched tight across its cheekbones, and where its nose should have been were just two ragged holes.

"Jack, look out!" Emily cried, for the lampir was moving towards him.

But before Jack could respond, it twisted a half-decayed arm around his neck and snapped its fangs so close to his cheek that Emily was sure it had bitten him. Jack struggled helplessly in the lampir's powerful grip, but then something strange happened: the lampir gave a roar of anger and released him, throwing him to the ground. Jack scrambled to his feet, a stunned look on his face. But there wasn't time to think about what this meant, because the lampir was turning on Ben. It fastened its claws around Ben's neck and bent its head to drink his blood.

But at that moment, Emily snatched up a piece of smouldering timber and hurled it at the lampir. Sparks flew like fireflies. Then the lampir burst into flame. A terrible smell of singed hair and burning dust filled the air as the creature dissolved into grey ash.

The friends looked around fearfully, searching the shadows for any more lampirs.

"That *had* to be the last one," Jack said eventually.

"We must go," Filip replied. He spotted the blue hat-box on the ground by the warehouse door, and hurried to pick it up. "We should put ze Dhampir Bell in here, out of sight. If we are carrying it through ze streets of London looking like this –" he gestured to his own sodden clothing – "then we might be arrested as thieves!"

With the Dhampir Bell safely stowed in the hat-box, Ben and Emily started to follow Filip. Then Emily realized Jack wasn't coming and she turned to see what he was doing.

"You go on ahead," Jack called. "There's something I need to do."

"What is it, Jack?" Ben asked.

"Henry," Jack replied simply.

He didn't need to elaborate further. With sober faces, the four friends trooped back to the warehouse door. It was still half-open. Jack picked up the candle that he'd tossed aside earlier and lit the wick from one of the smouldering pieces of timber which littered the dockside. Holding the light in front of him, he led the sombre procession into the dark warehouse.

Packing cases and crates loomed on every side and cinders and ash crunched underfoot – the remains of vanquished lampirs. Even though she was sure there were no more lampirs inside, Emily found her heart pounding. They reached the clearing in the middle of the room, and Captain Marek's body. Jack held the candle high and the shadows around them melted away as shadows should.

Then a small sound came out of the darkness. They all paused, listening. Was it a lampir?

Then a whimper broke the silence. "That's no lampir – that's Henry!" Jack exclaimed. He darted towards the sound, with the others hot on his heels.

Henry was sitting propped against a wooden crate, his chin on his chest and his clothes torn. Blood streamed from wounds on his face, neck, arms and hands – but he was alive!

"Henry, me old mate!" Jack cried with a huge grin.

Emily found she was trembling with relief and happiness as she and Jack helped Henry to his feet. He could stand, though he was weak, and as they made their way out of the warehouse he told them what had happened.

"Them lampirs were going to drink my blood," he said. "They was tearing at me clothes and biting me. I thought I was a goner. But then all of a sudden this bell started ringing and they just dropped me. Before I knew it, I was on me own. They'd all gone off, groanin' and moanin' after the bell."

Emily glanced at Jack. "Thank goodness you rang it when you did," she said.

Jack grimaced. "I thought you was dead," he confessed to Henry, as they emerged from the warehouse and began to make their way along the wharf. "I only rang the bell then, because I was so angry."

"Cor, you saved me!" Henry gazed up at Jack with hero-worship in his eyes. "Thanks, Jack."

Jack tousled the little lad's hair. "Don't mention it, mate," he replied happily.

An hour later Ben, Jack, Emily and Filip were standing outside the watch and clock shop in Tiler's Alley. They had taken Henry straight to Jack's old haunt, the Admiral Nelson inn, to see whether Bill, the landlord, would let them have some bandages for Henry's wounds.

Bill had taken one look at the boy, however, and stoutly refused to do anything less than take Henry in and give him a home.

"Too many waifs and strays round these docks," Bill had declared, giving Jack a knowing look. "Someone's got to do something about it. I know Molly used to lend you boys a hand – give you food and such like. Well, I'm right shamed that I didn't do more meself."

He bent down and peered into Henry's face, his eyes twinkling and his bushy grey beard almost tickling the lad's nose. "How would you like ter come and live with me?"

Henry's face lit up. "Yes, please, Bill!"

So it was settled. The friends had seen Henry patched up and then left him and Bill at the door of the Admiral Nelson, both of them beaming with happiness. Now it was time to say goodbye to Filip Cinska. He was going to take the Dhampir Bell back to Poland as soon as he could book passage on a ship bound for the Baltic.

"Goodbye, Filip, and good luck!" Emily said, giving the little Polish man a huge hug and planting a kiss on his cheek.

The boys, however, were more restrained. Ben shook Filip's hand formally, and Jack, feeling hugely conscious of what a gentleman might do, copied Ben.

But Filip was having none of their English reserve. "You need to learn how ze Polish say farewell!" he declared. And with that he pulled them all – Ben, Jack and Emily – into his wiry arms for a hug. "I will miss you, my friends," he said, his voice muffled.

Behind him the door to his lodging house crashed open. Widow Kaminski stomped out on to the doorstep and glared at them from beneath her thick black eyebrows.

"Hugging in the streets!" She tutted in disgust. "Whatever next!"

Filip laughed loudly. Then he released the three friends and threw his arms around the surprised widow. "Dear lady," he exclaimed. "I think that I will even miss you!"

CHAPTER TWENTY-SIX

The hansom carried the three friends into Bedford Square and Ben gazed at the house with a feeling of lightness in his heart. There was a holly wreath tied to the door knocker with a bright scarlet ribbon, and all the lights were on indoors, making the windows glow.

"Home," Ben said softly. "Doesn't it look wonderful?"

"It does," Jack said with a grin. "But I'd rather look at it from the inside if you don't mind. It's freezing out 'ere!" He tipped back his head and sniffed the air. "Reckon I can smell snow. . ."

Ben laughed. "You can't *smell* snow," he teased.

"Course you can!" Jack responded indignantly.

Emily shook her head, laughing as she stepped down from the hansom. "You're just cold, tired, wet and hungry," she said. "And your imagination's playing tricks on you, Jack."

But Jack shook his head. "Wet and hungry or not, I

can smell snow," he said firmly. "We're going to have a white Christmas."

"Talking of our wet clothes," Emily said, looking worried, "how are we going to explain things to Mrs Mills?"

Ben paid the hansom cab driver and turned to gaze up at the front door again. "We'll just have to sneak in," he said, "and get changed before she notices."

They hurried up the steps, pushed the door open – and walked straight into a commotion.

Mrs Mills stood with her back to the front door, shooing Tillet, the housemaid, towards the drawing-room. For some reason, Tillet had an enormous slice of cheese in her hands! Meanwhile, Evans was scurrying around in a blind panic, lugging with her something that looked like a horseshoe, but which on closer inspection turned to be a big iron rat-trap. Cook was standing on a chair in the middle of the hallway, her skirts held up so high that Ben was quite shocked to see not only her sturdy calves, but also the frill at the bottom of her knee-length bloomers. He looked away hurriedly.

"What on earth is going on?" Ben asked.

At the unexpected sound of his voice, Cook gave a whoop of fright and nearly fell off the chair, Tillet screamed and ran into the drawing-room with her cheese, and Evans dropped the rat-trap with a clatter and threw her apron up to cover her face.

Mrs Mills turned to the three friends with her hands

on her hips. "You may well ask, Master Benedict," she said sternly. "And I'll tell you. There's a rat in the house – a big one, too!"

"I see. . ." Ben eyed the rat-trap. "Well, that contraption looks as if it'll do the job."

"That's what we're hoping," Mrs Mills agreed. She turned back to the housemaids. "Come along, now. It's Christmas Eve and we've got quite enough to do without all this nonsense!"

Christmas Eve! Ben, Jack and Emily exchanged thrilled glances. Then, before Mrs Mills had time to notice their bedraggled appearance, they hurried upstairs to their rooms.

"Christmas Eve," Emily whispered, as they paused on the landing together. "I'm so excited, aren't you, Jack?"

"Fit to burst," Jack replied, beaming. "I ain't never had a proper Christmas before. Not one with presents, and lovely food, and all the decorations you've got here. I can't believe I'm going to wake up to all that tomorrow!"

But wake up to all that he did. And he knew the moment he opened his eyes that he'd been right about the snow. There was a strange, bluish light in his bedroom and it was unusually quiet! Everything seemed muffled, as if he had cotton wool stuffed in his ears.

Jack threw back the bedclothes and dashed to the window. Bedford Square sparkled and glittered below him, covered with a thick layer of crisp white snow. With a whoop of delight, Jack threw on some clothes and ran along the landing knocking on bedroom doors.

"Ben, wake up! There's snow. . . Emily, come on! It's Christmas Day. Come and see the snow!"

He pelted downstairs and ran headlong into Mrs Mills, who chuckled as he grabbed her by the hands and twirled her round.

"Merry Christmas, Mrs M!" he cried.

Ben and Emily came pounding down the stairs behind him. Emily's eyes were shining with excitement as she wound a scarf around her neck and slipped into her coat. Ben laughed and snatched up a cap which he jammed on his head. Then they all tumbled outside, scrunching through the snow, scooping up handfuls and making snowballs.

Jack gasped as one hit him square in the middle of his chest. He looked up to see that Emily had thrown it! "Great shot," he exclaimed, and hurled one right back at her.

Attracted by the happy sound of their laughter, other children began to pour out of neighbouring houses, shrieking with delight. Soon a full-scale snow-battle was in progress, with snowballs flying through the air and hitting their targets with alarming accuracy.

Mrs Mills watched them all from the front door, shaking her head and laughing. "Don't get chilled, now," she warned. "I'd better go and speak to Cook about making hot chocolate for you when you come in!"

Later that day the three friends sat by a roaring log fire in the drawing-room, recovering from an enormous dinner of roast goose followed by a sweet and steamy plum pudding. The warm air smelled deliciously of cinnamon cakes and pine cones. Ben had lit the candles on the Christmas tree; it looked beautiful over in the corner by the window, its glass baubles glinting in the flickering light.

Outside it was dark. Snow had begun to fall again, whispering down to fill in the footprints of the morning's snowball fight. Church bells rang out all across the city and the three friends could hear their neighbour, old Major Carstairs, singing "O Come, All Ye Faithful" to the accompaniment of his wife's tinkling piano.

Jack sat back in one of the over-stuffed armchairs. He smiled across at his best friends, who were standing by the Christmas tree. Emily was busily heaping Ben's arms with presents wrapped in shiny gold paper. Jack reflected that he'd never felt so happy in his life. He was warm and well-fed, and now that he, Ben and Emily had defeated the lampir plague, everything was right with the world.

Emily came dancing across to him and dropped a present in his lap. "Merry Christmas, Jack!" she said.

He was amazed. "For me?" he queried. Emily nodded and Jack read the label. It was from Ben. Thrilled, he unwrapped it to reveal a brand new, leather-bound copy of the latest Charles Dickens novel. Jack ran his fingers over it, smiling. "Thank you, Ben. . ." he murmured, feeling rather over-awed.

Emily, meanwhile, was busy with a present of her own. She had knelt down on the hearth-rug to untie a length of green silk ribbon from a big square box. "Wonder what it is?" she said softly. "It feels heavy. . ."

As the ribbon came undone, the lid of the box burst open – and like a macabre jack-in-the-box Uncle Jerzy's severed hand sprang out. It grabbed at Emily's throat.

Emily screamed and threw herself backwards so that the hand caught her blouse and not her neck. Jack was by her side in an instant, reaching for the hand, but he couldn't get a grip on the decaying flesh.

Startled by Emily's scream, Ben dropped his armful of presents and turned to see what was happening. As soon as he saw the hand, he launched himself across the room. He managed to seize hold of the writhing fingers, but it was a struggle to hang on. His own fingers kept slipping, and the long black nails of the hand were sharp! At last he and Jack got a grip and together they wrenched the hand away from Emily. It fell to the floor, and they all watched in horror as it scuttled away from them, towards the pile of presents.

"Quick!" Jack gasped. "We have to set fire to it."

He dashed to the Christmas tree and grabbed one of the candles. The tiny flame flickered as Jack ducked towards the presents. Ben hurried to help him, tossing boxes and parcels aside in a frenzied search for the hand.

"There it is!" Emily yelled, pointing.

But at that moment, the drawing-room door swung open. "There's what, my dear?" asked Mrs Mills.

Emily stared at Mrs Mills. "Er, the rat!" she exclaimed, quickly. "I saw the rat, Mrs Mills – it was huge!"

"Oh, my life! I'll get the rat-trap," Mrs Mills cried, and rushed from the room.

"Quick," said Ben, "we've got to find the hand before she comes back!"

They rifled through the piles of presents, picking up cushions and peering under footstools and sofas. But the hand was nowhere to be seen.

Eventually, Jack sighed and shook his head. "Reckon it must've gone," he said.

Ben nodded. "It probably slipped into shadow-form and went under the front door, like last time."

"I hope so!" Emily said with a shudder.

"We just have to be thankful that it's only a hand and not a whole lampir," Jack pointed out. "A hand I think we can deal with – if it ever comes back."

Ben nodded. "And even if *we* don't," he added with a smile, "Mrs Mills's rat-trap certainly will!"

"Come on," said Emily, firmly. "It's Christmas Day. There are more important things to do than worry about a silly old lampir hand."

She picked up two of the biggest presents, glimmering

in their gold wrapping paper, and handed one each to Ben and Jack.

"Merry Christmas!" she declared, happily.

THE
DEVIL'S TRADE

THE SIGN OF THE
ANGEL

ALAN MACDONALD

Will felt the cold blade of a pocket knife pressed to his throat.

"We don't take kindly to spies," breathed the undertaker. "Their tongues will be wagging. Better to cut 'em out and feed 'em to the fishes."

Will swears on his life to keep the smugglers' secret and his tongue is spared. Now he's caught up in a dark and treacherous world where he finally learns the truth about his father's *heroic* death...

Will is desperate to gain admittance to the smugglers' dangerous underworld but first he must prove his loyalty. Someone has been passing information to the Revenue men and Will is high on the list of suspects. The smugglers have their own ways of dealing with traitors and Will knows that he must find the real culprit before it's too late. It's not for nothing that smuggling is known as the Devil's Trade...

LOOK OUT FOR

THIS GRIPPING SERIES...